MIND THIEF

BY DAVID ORME

STONE ARCH BOOKS
www.stonearchbooks.com

First published in the United States in 2009
by Stone Arch Books
151 Good Counsel Drive, P.O. Box 669
Mankato, Minnesota 56002
www.stonearchbooks.com

Copyright © 2007 Ransom Publishing Ltd.
Illustration copyright © 2007 Peter Richardson

Library of Congress Cataloging-in-Publication Data
Orme, David, 1948 Mar. 1–
   [Boffin Boy and the Wizard of Edo]
   Mind Thief / by David Orme; illustrated by Peter Richardson.
   p. cm. — (Billy Blaster)
   Originally published: Boffin Boy and the Wizard of Edo. Watlington: Ransom, 2007.
   ISBN 978-1-4342-1276-4 (library binding)
   1. Graphic novels. [1. Graphic novels. 2. Heroes—Fiction. 3. Science fiction.]
I. Richardson, Peter, 1965– ill. II. Title.
PZ7.7.O76Min 2009
741.5'973—dc22   2008031450

Summary:
Billy Blaster and his friend Wu Hoo are tracking a dangerous new foe – a wizard who
is stealing the minds of scientists. But the hunted becomes the hunter and suddenly the
wizard kidnaps Wu Hoo! Billy needs help, so he calls on his friend Rika. The two make a
great team in their search for Wu Hoo, but time is running out.

Creative Director: Heather Kindseth
Graphic Designer: Carla Zetina-Yglesias

BILLY BLASTER

written by
DAVID ORME

illustrated by
PETER RICHARDSON

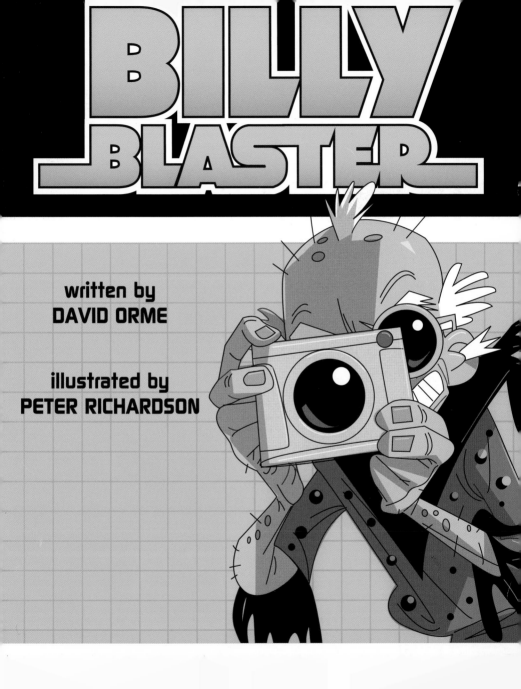

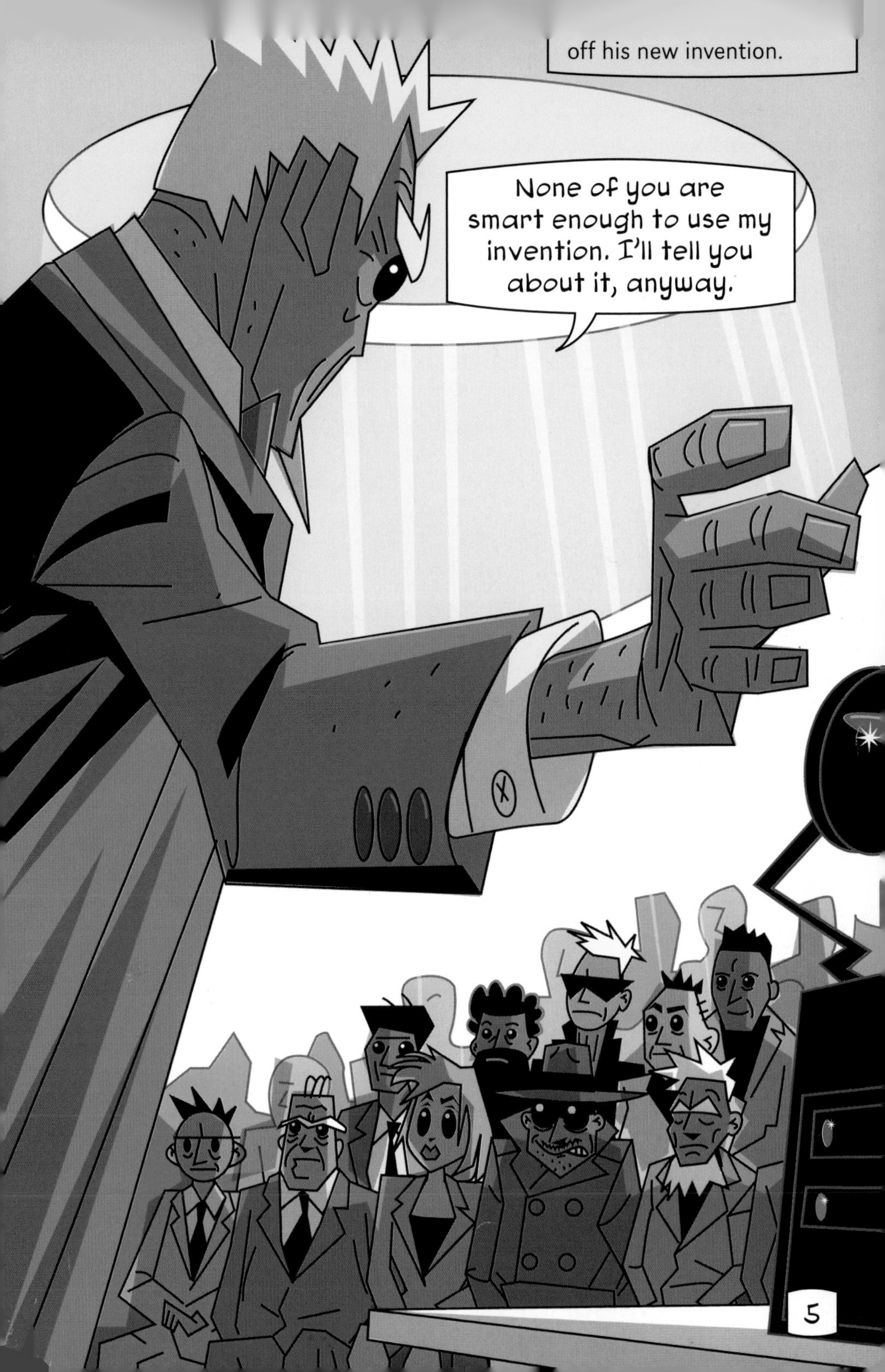
off his new invention.
None of you are smart enough to use my invention. I'll tell you about it, anyway.

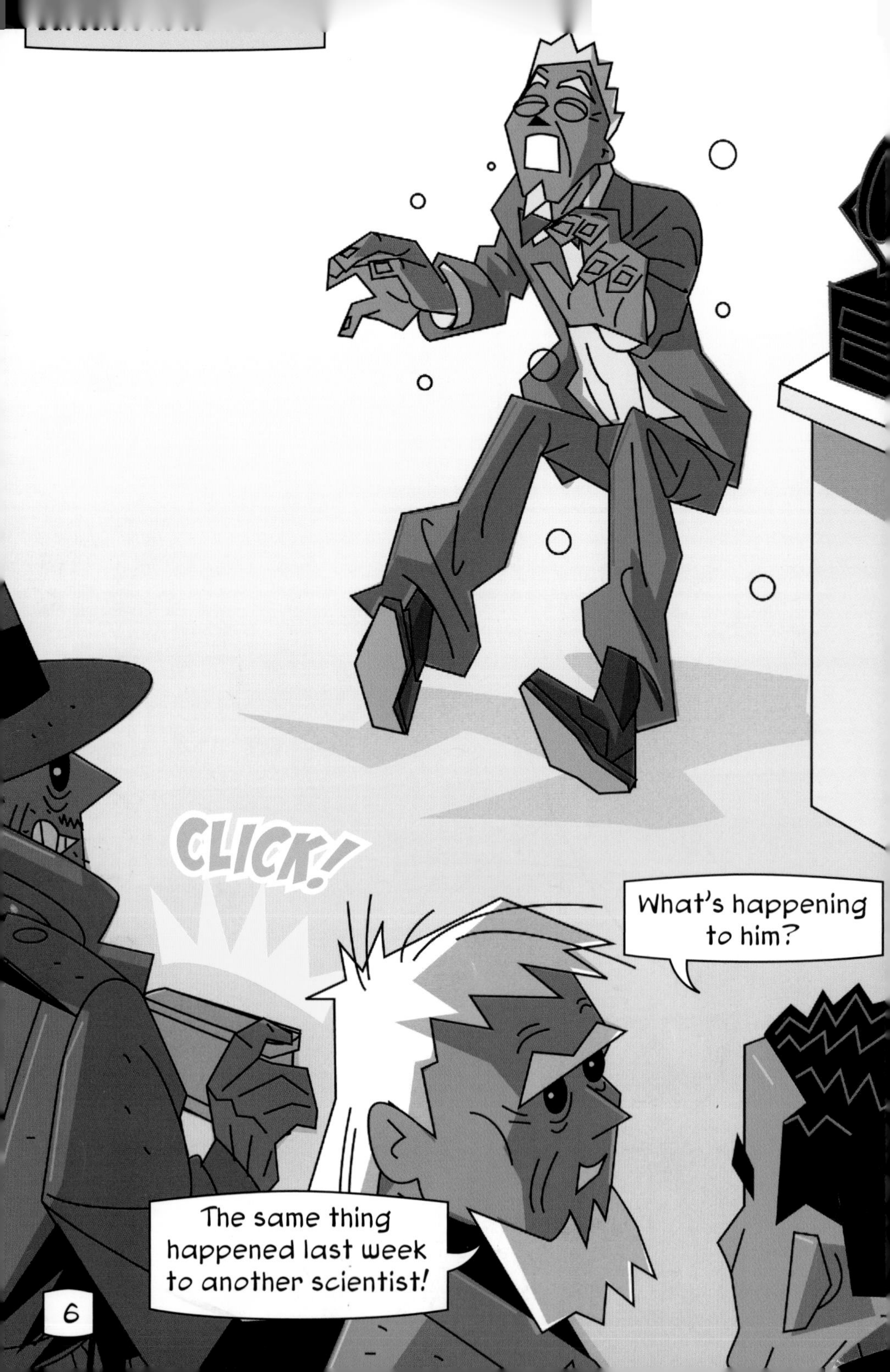
CLICK!
What's happening to him?
The same thing happened last week to another scientist!

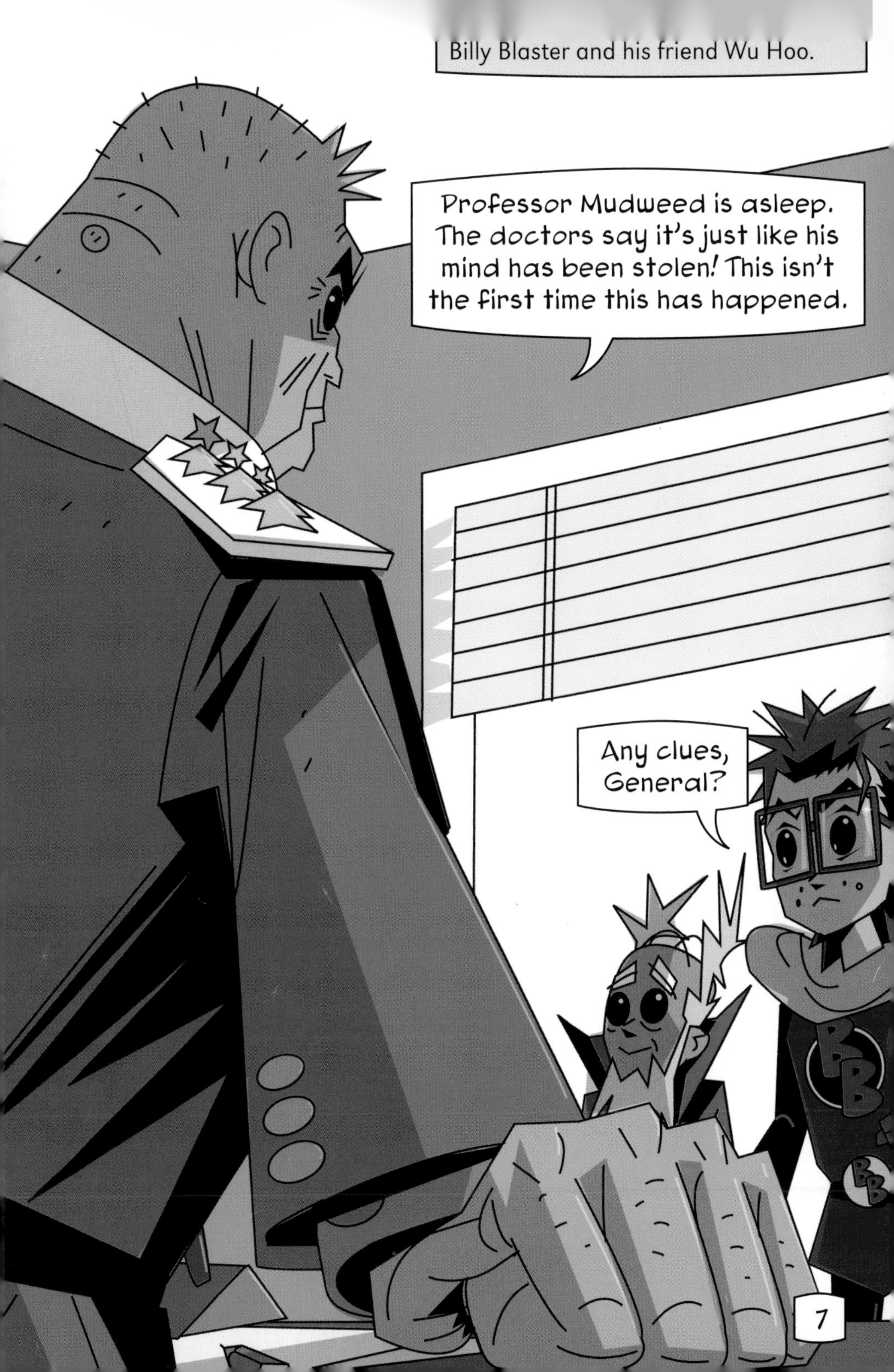
Billy Blaster and his friend Wu Hoo.
Professor Mudweed is asleep. The doctors say it's just like his mind has been stolen! This isn't the first time this has happened.
Any clues, General?

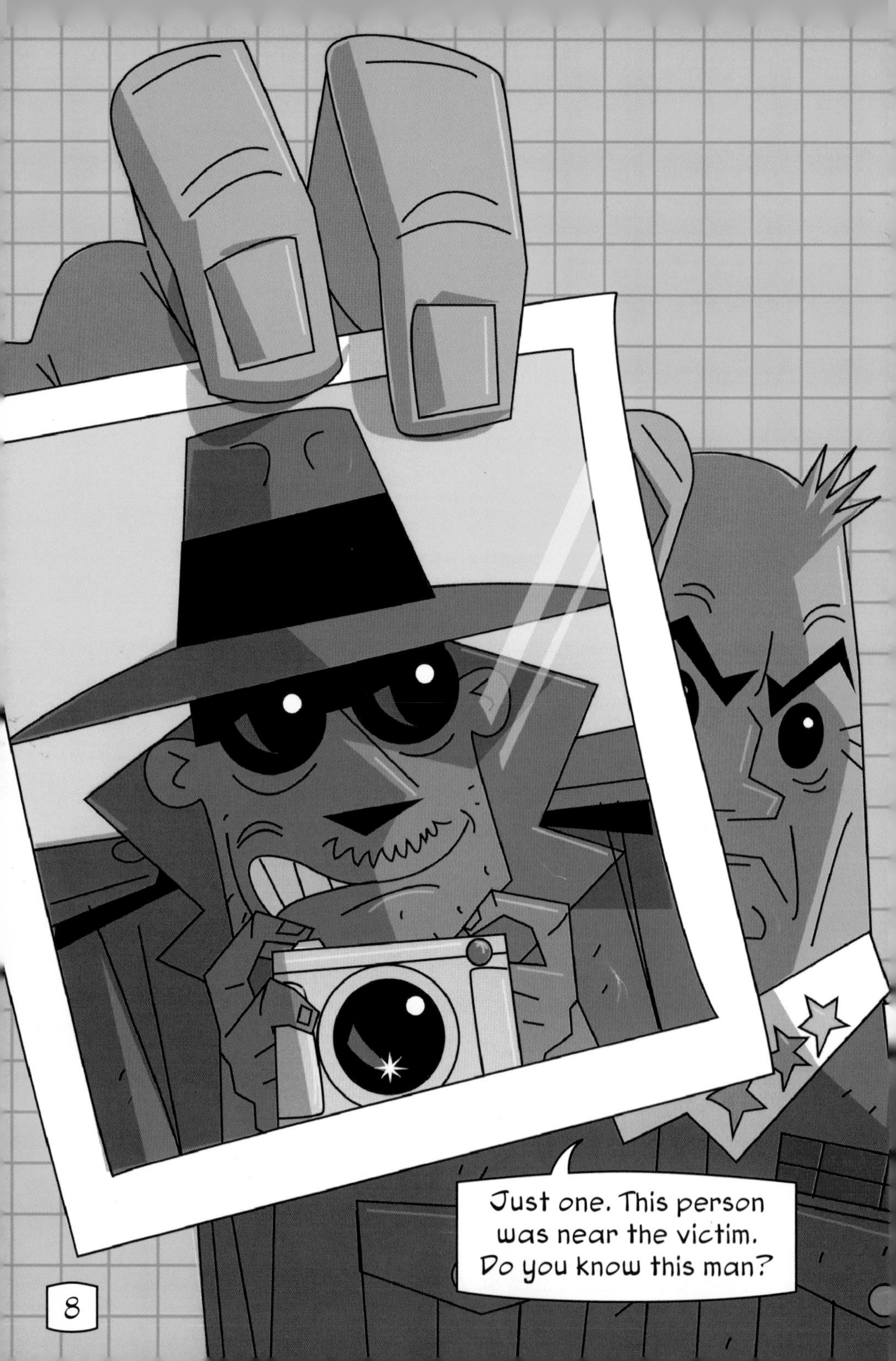
Just one. This person was near the victim. Do you know this man?

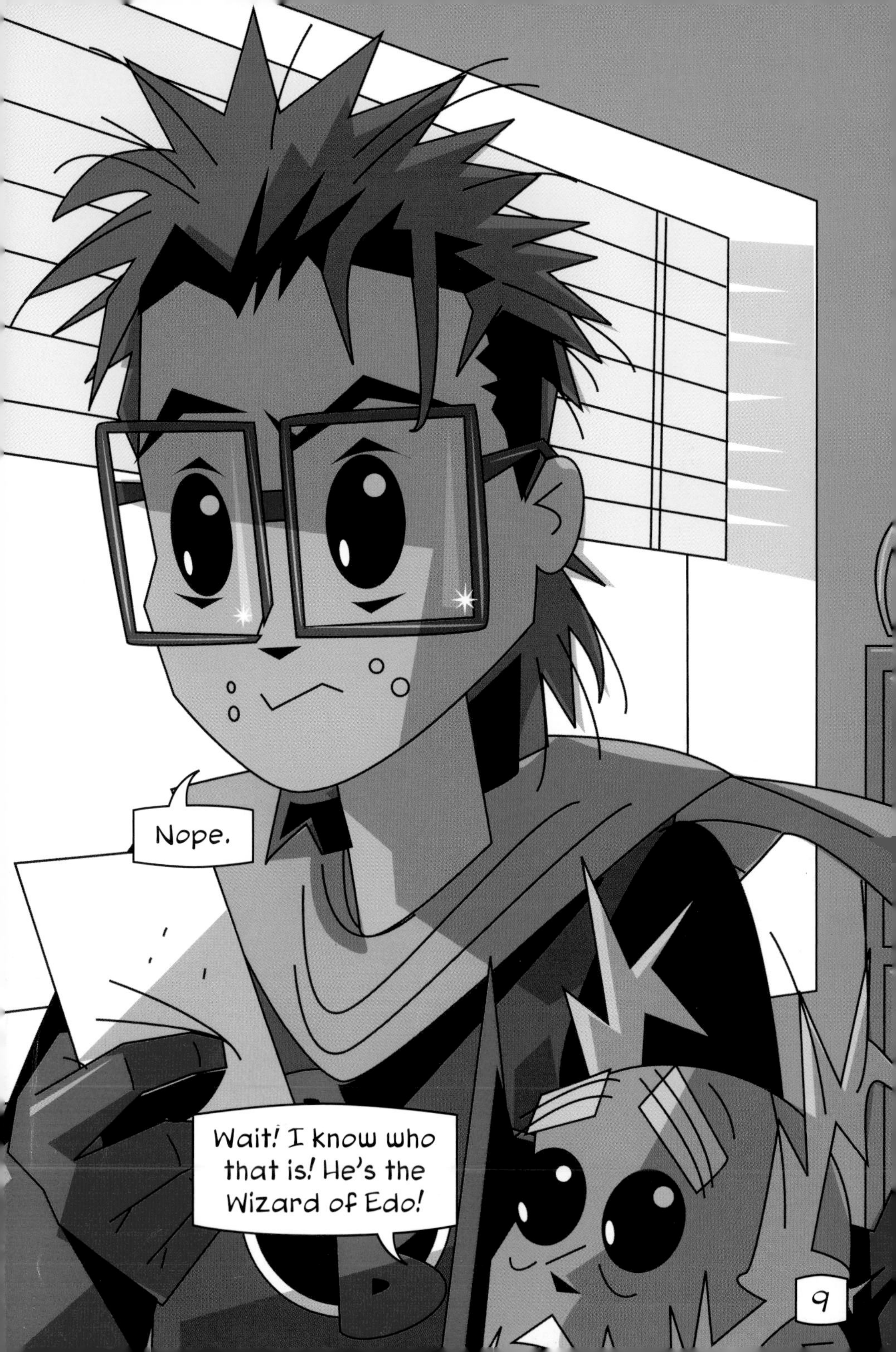
Nope.
Wait! I know who that is! He's the Wizard of Edo!

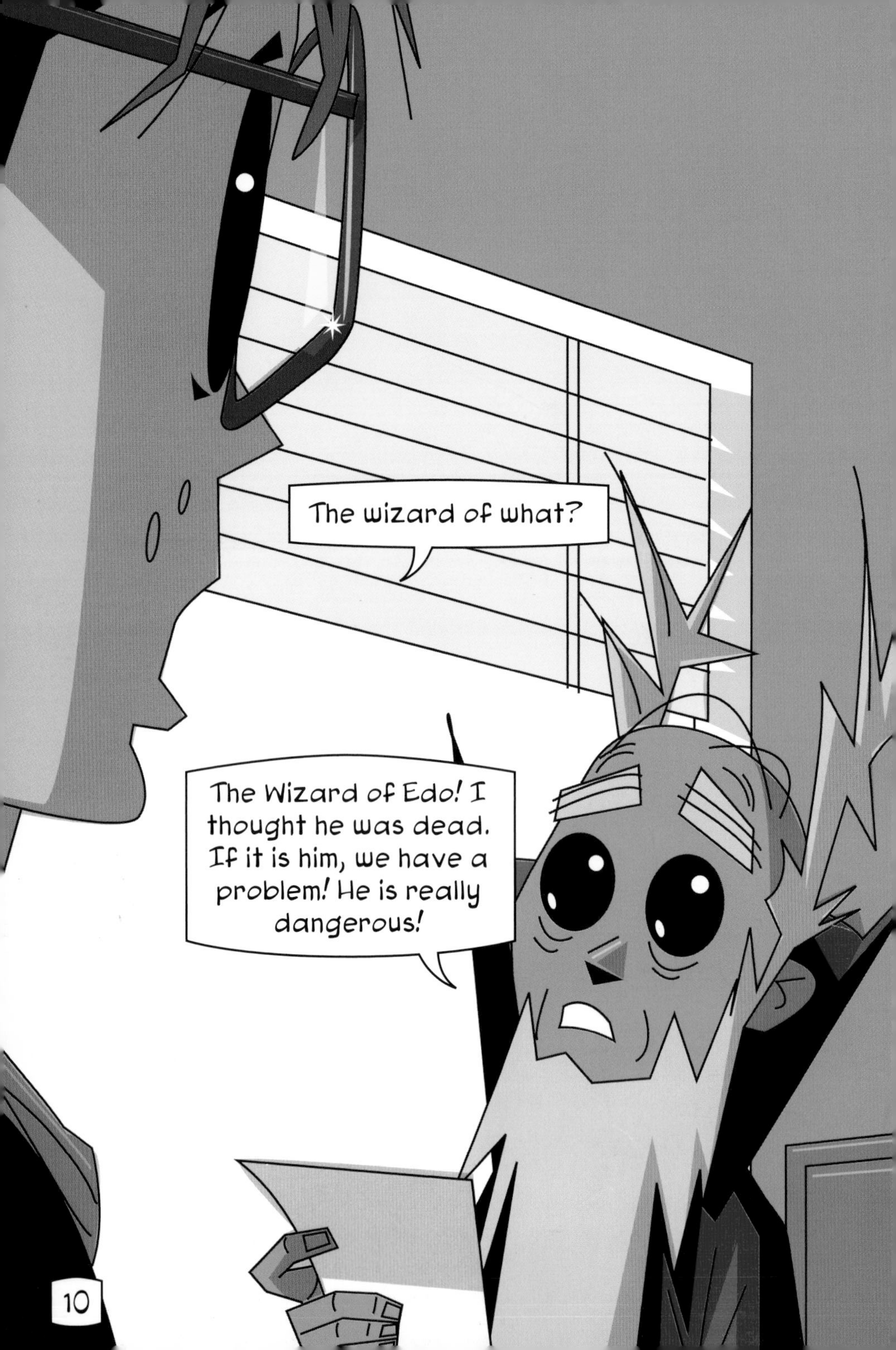
The wizard of what?
The Wizard of Edo! I thought he was dead. If it is him, we have a problem! He is really dangerous!

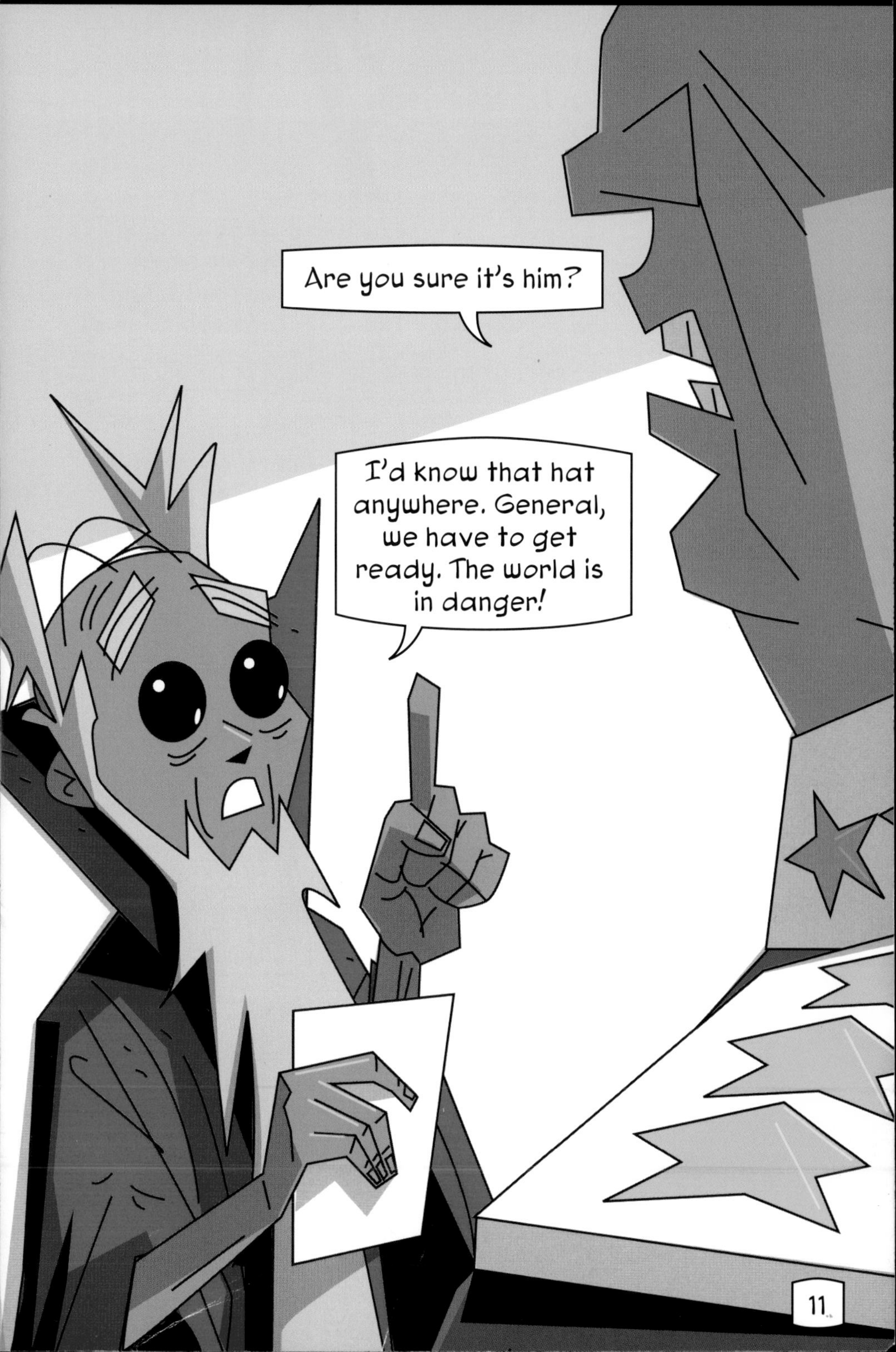
Are you sure it's him?
I'd know that hat anywhere. General, we have to get ready. The world is in danger!

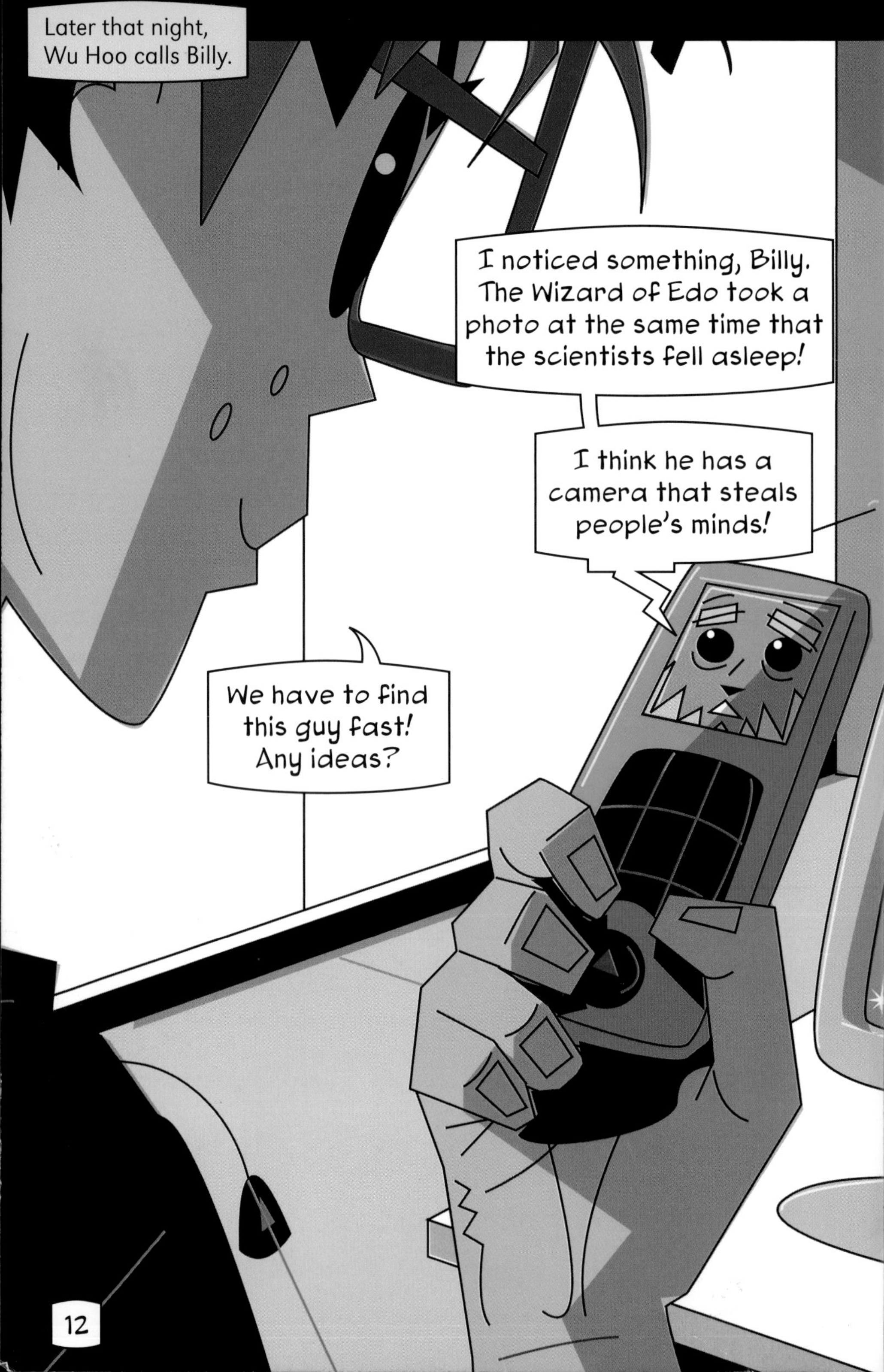

Later that night, Wu Hoo calls Billy.
I noticed something, Billy. The Wizard of Edo took a photo at the same time that the scientists fell asleep!
I think he has a camera that steals people's minds!
We have to find this guy fast! Any ideas?

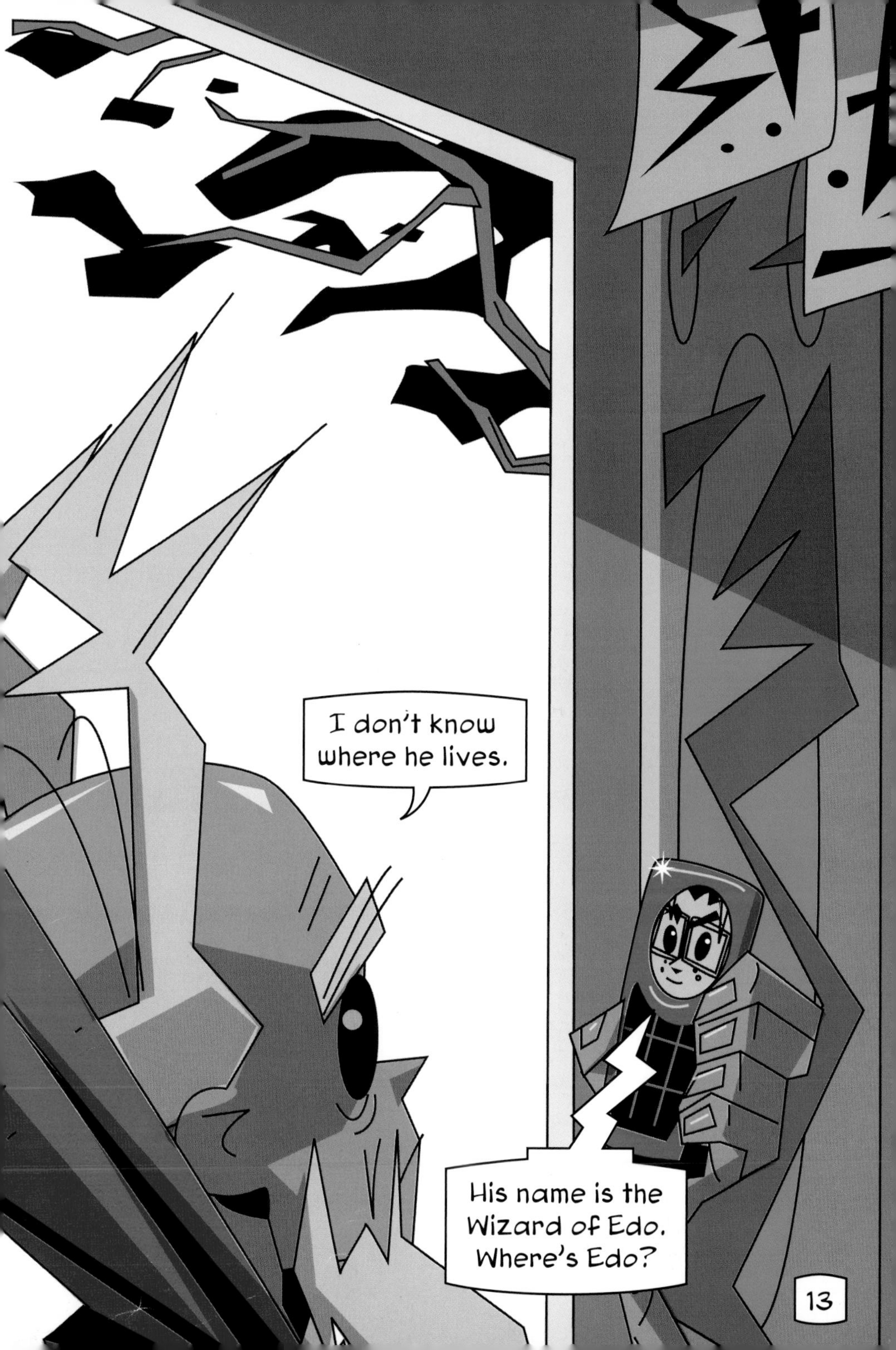
I don't know where he lives.
His name is the Wizard of Edo. Where's Edo?

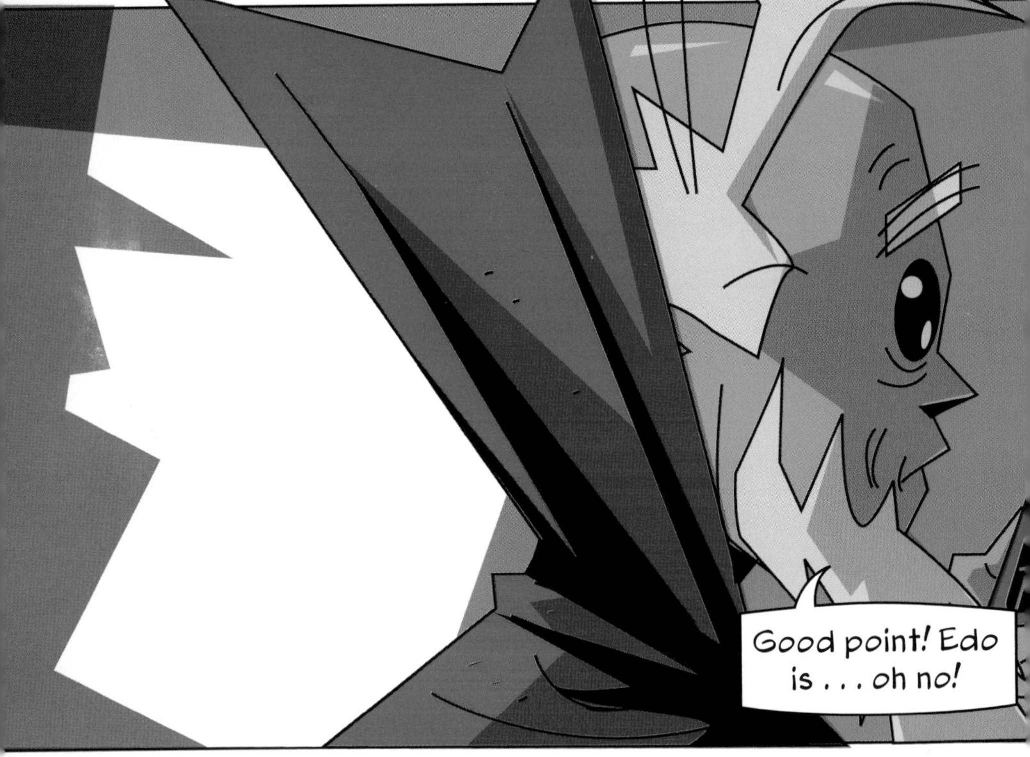
Good point! Edo is . . . oh no!

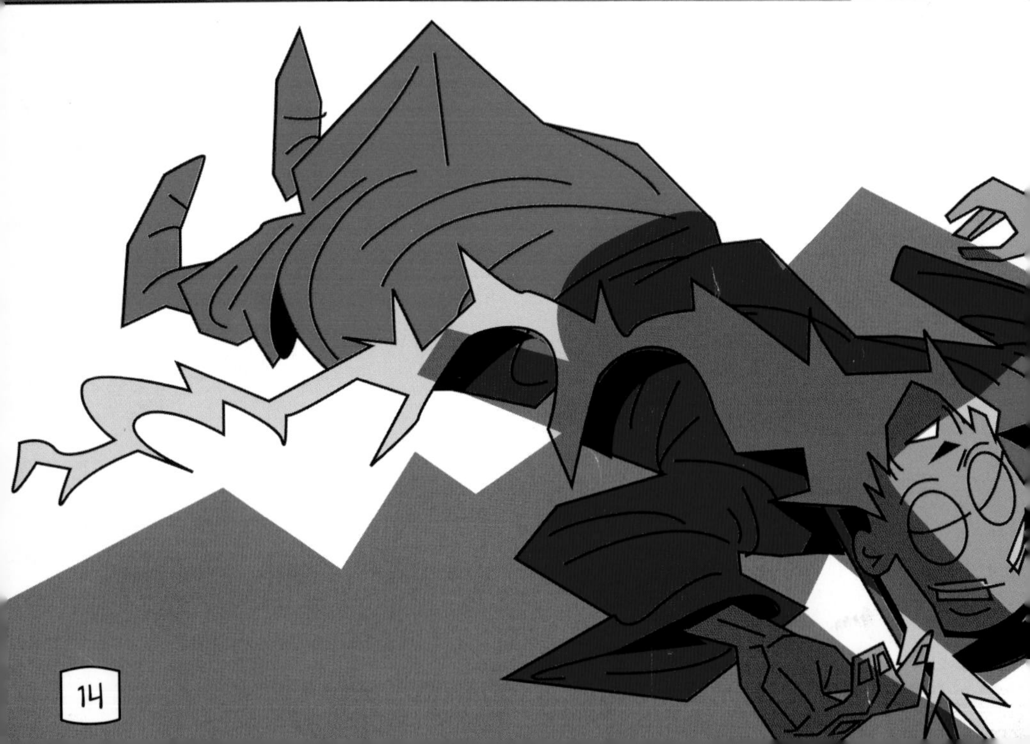

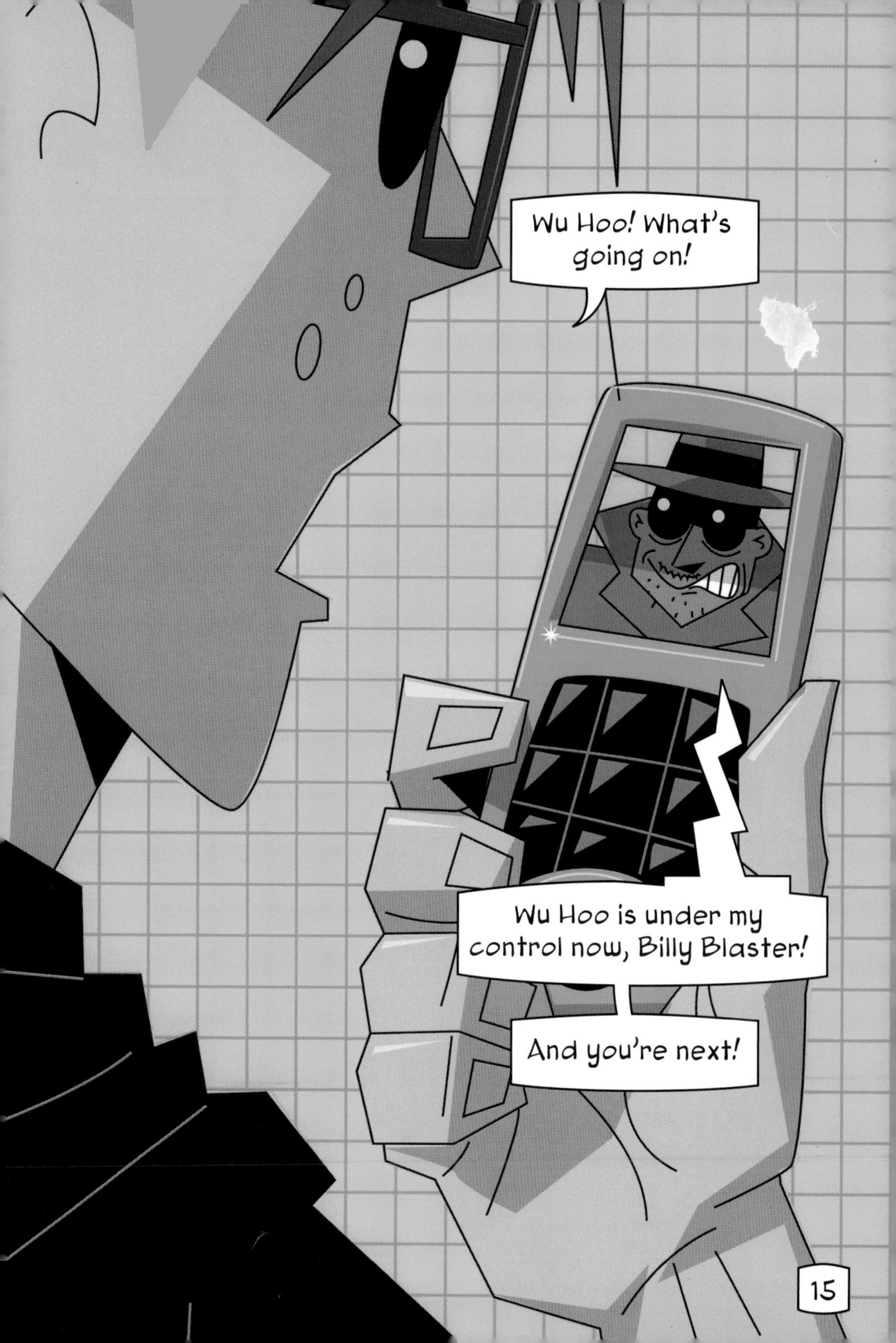
Wu Hoo! What's going on!
Wu Hoo is under my control now, Billy Blaster!
And you're next!

The Wizard has stolen Wu Hoo's mind! At least Wu Hoo's body is safe in the hospital.
It says here that Edo is the old name for Tokyo. Maybe I should visit my friend Rika in Japan. But first I have to invent something!

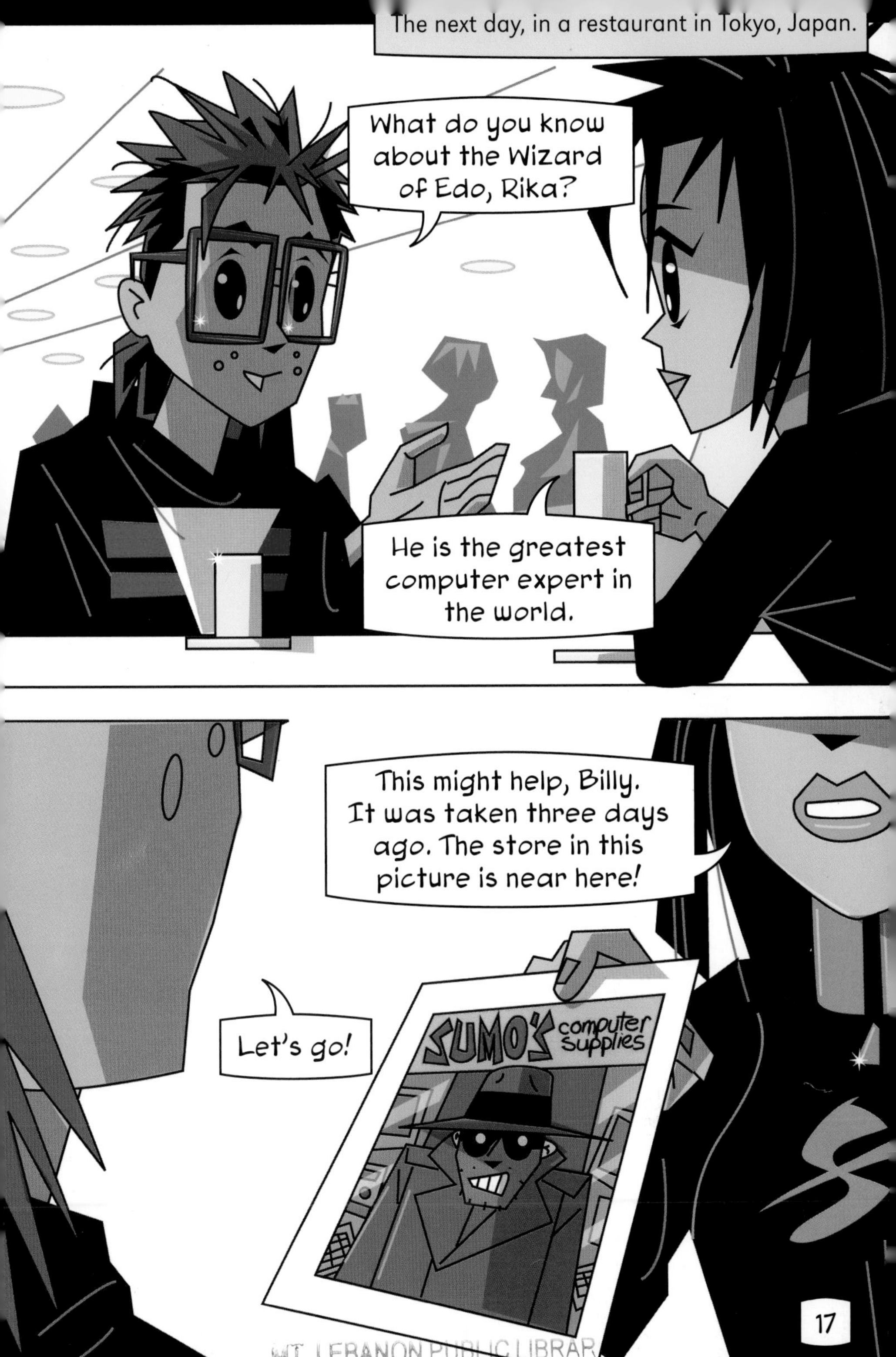
The next day, in a restaurant in Tokyo, Japan.
What do you know about the Wizard of Edo, Rika?
He is the greatest computer expert in the world.
This might help, Billy. It was taken three days ago. The store in this picture is near here!
Let's go!
SUMO'S computer supplies

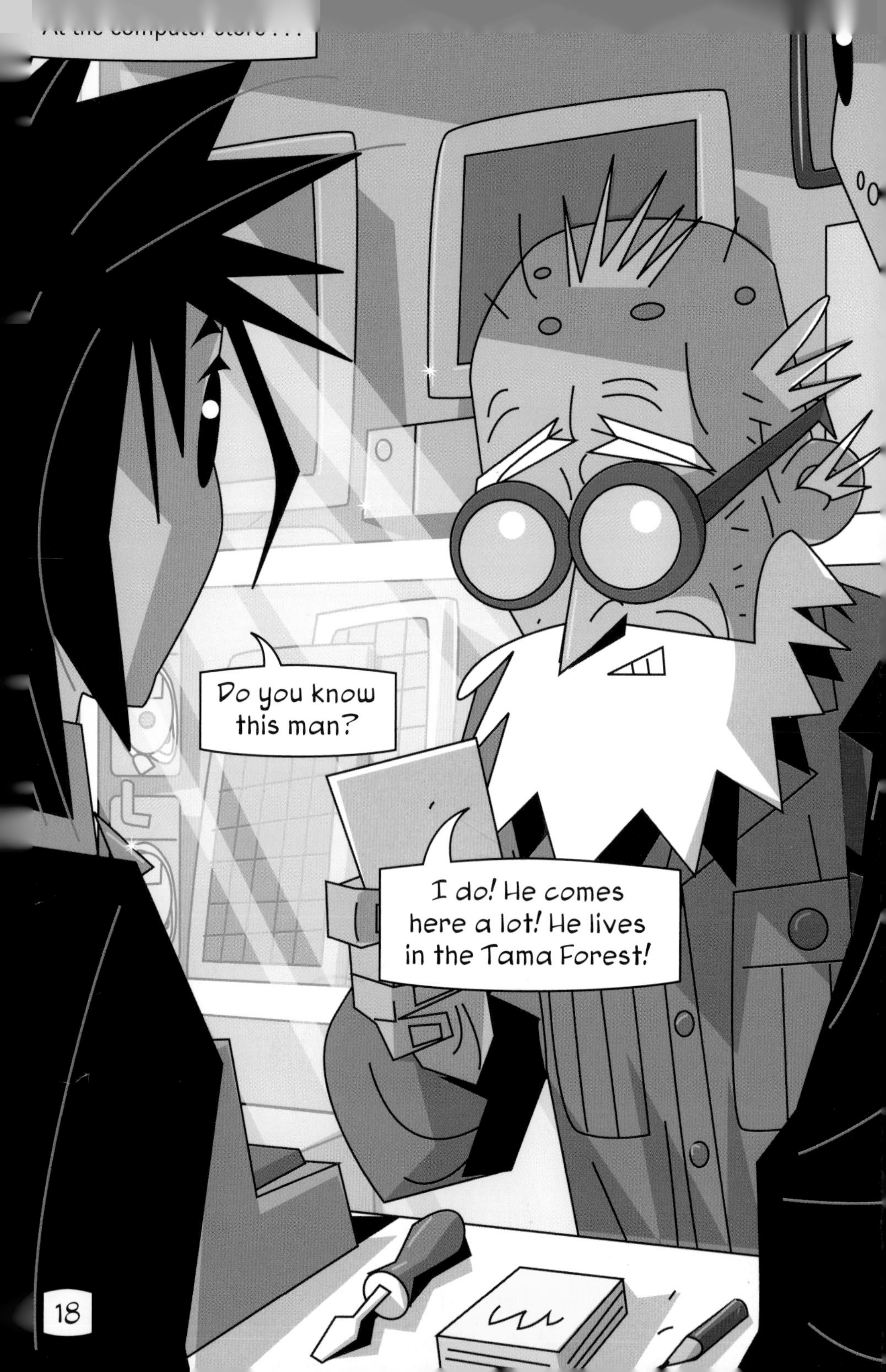
Do you know this man?
I do! He comes here a lot! He lives in the Tama Forest!

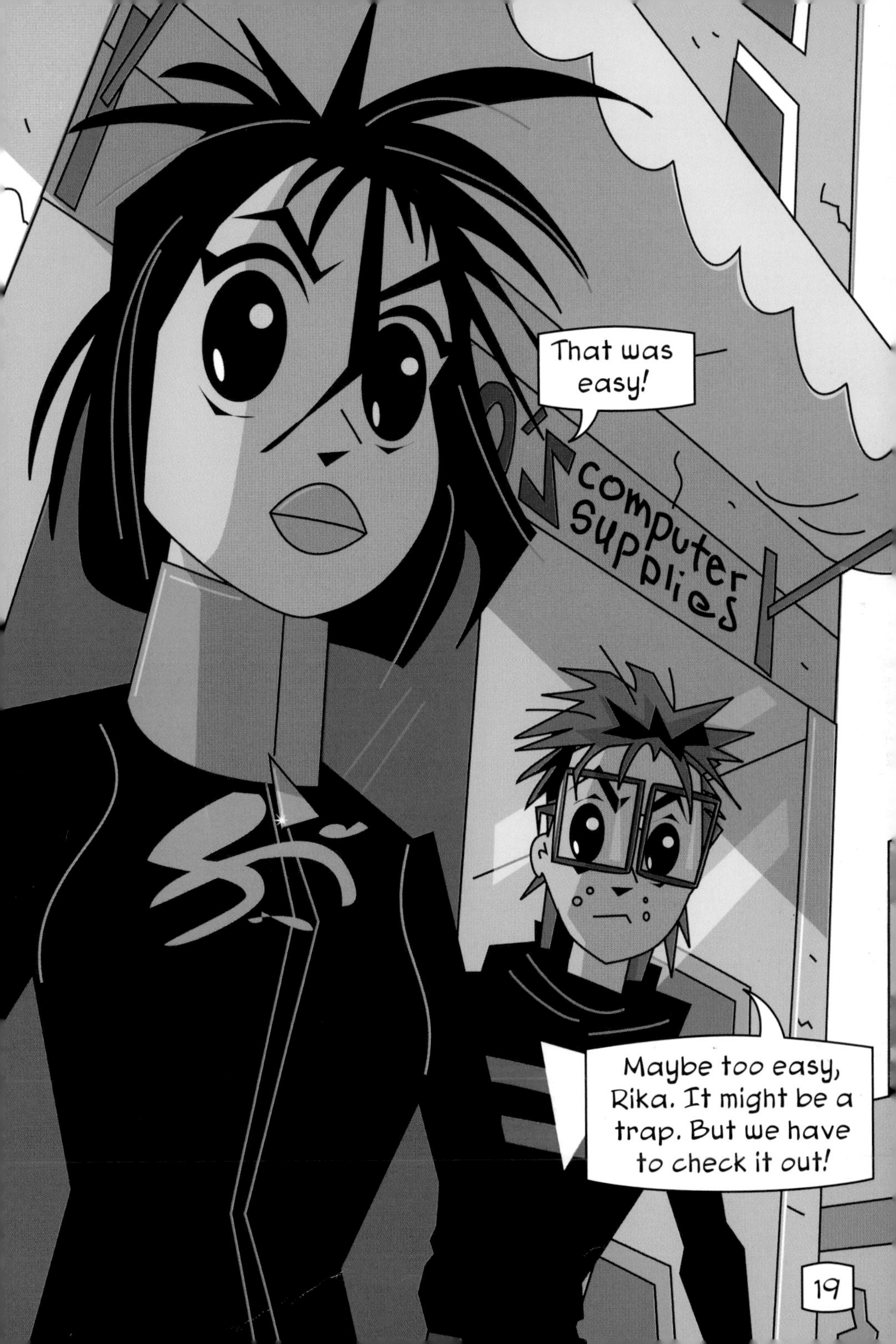
That was easy!
D's computer supplies
Maybe too easy, Rika. It might be a trap. But we have to check it out!

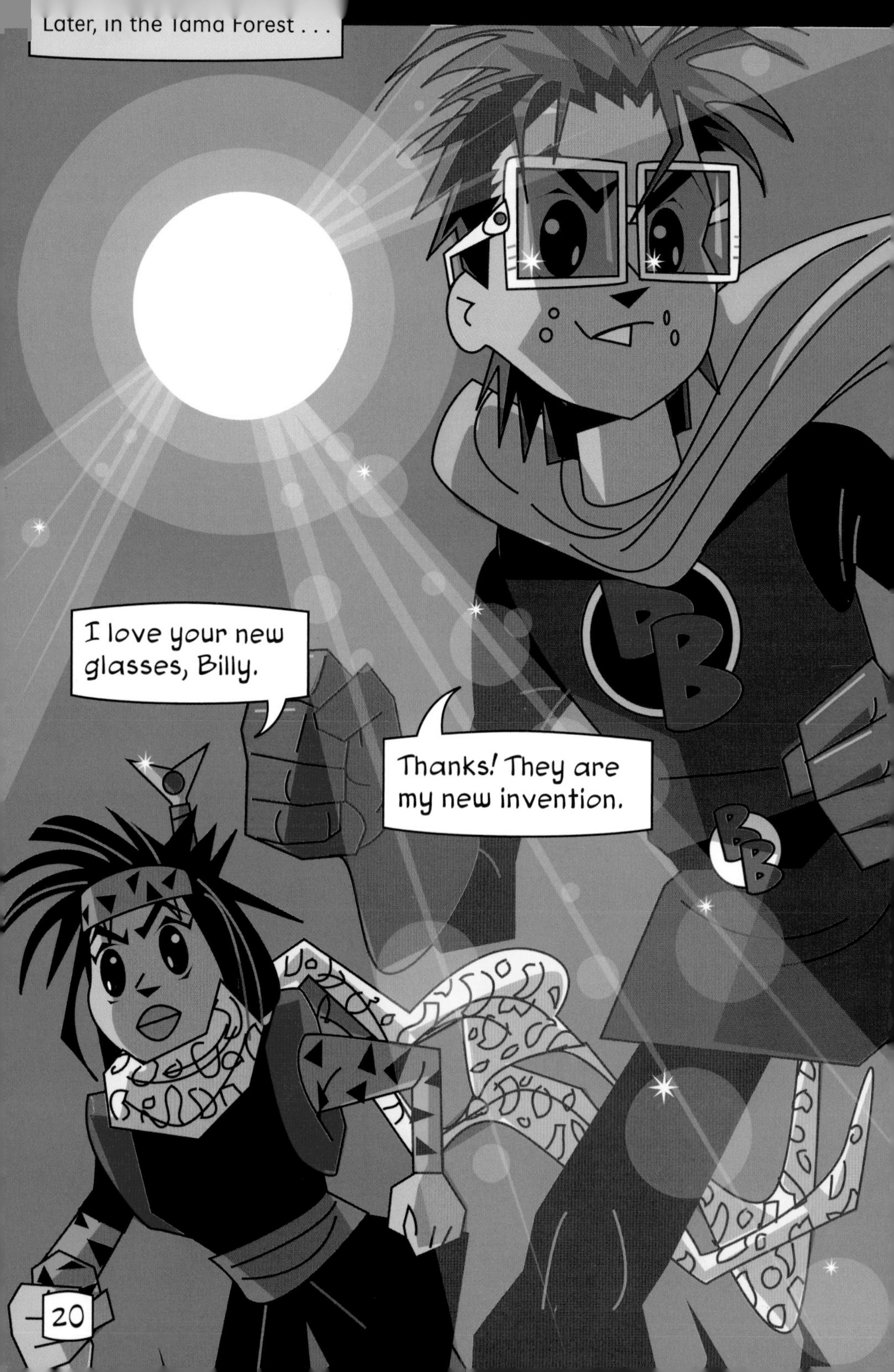
Later, in the Tama Forest . . .
I love your new glasses, Billy.
Thanks! They are my new invention.
BB
BB

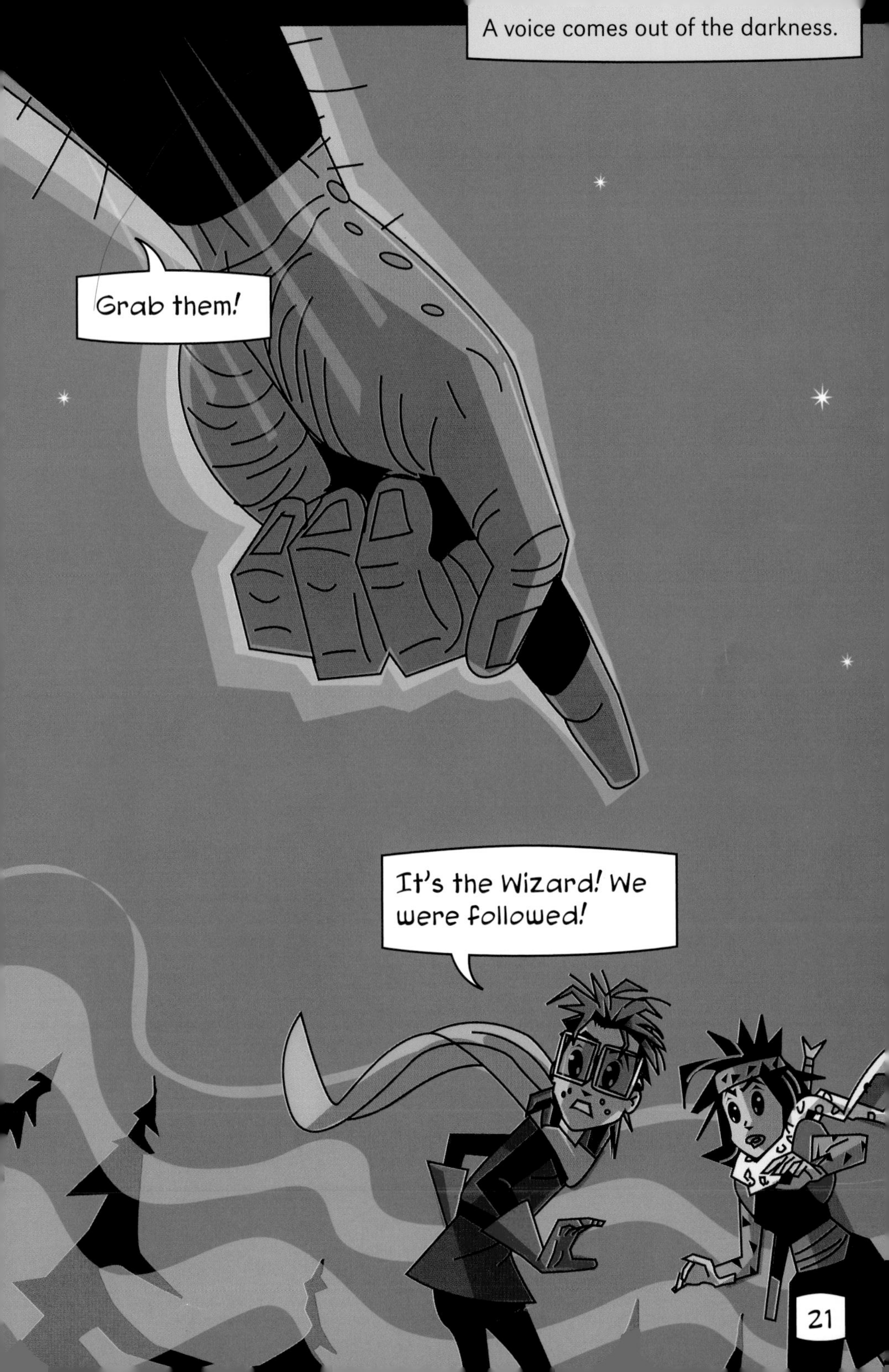
A voice comes out of the darkness.
Grab them!
It's the Wizard! We were followed!

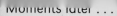

You're the man from the computer store!

I thought it would be hard to steal your mind, Billy Blaster. But you made it easy for me!

Tie them up and bring them back to the store!

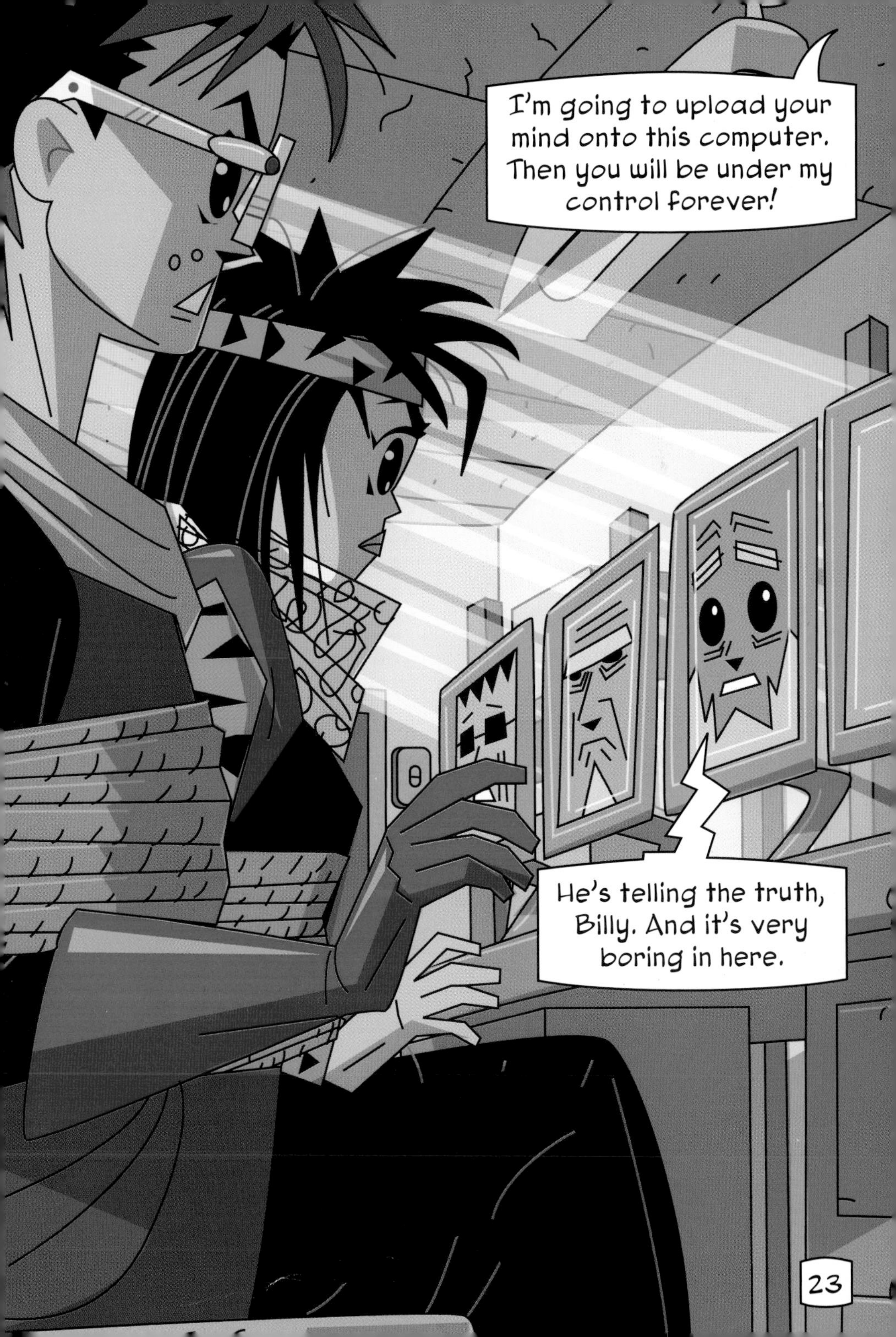
I'm going to upload your mind onto this computer. Then you will be under my control forever!
He's telling the truth, Billy. And it's very boring in here.

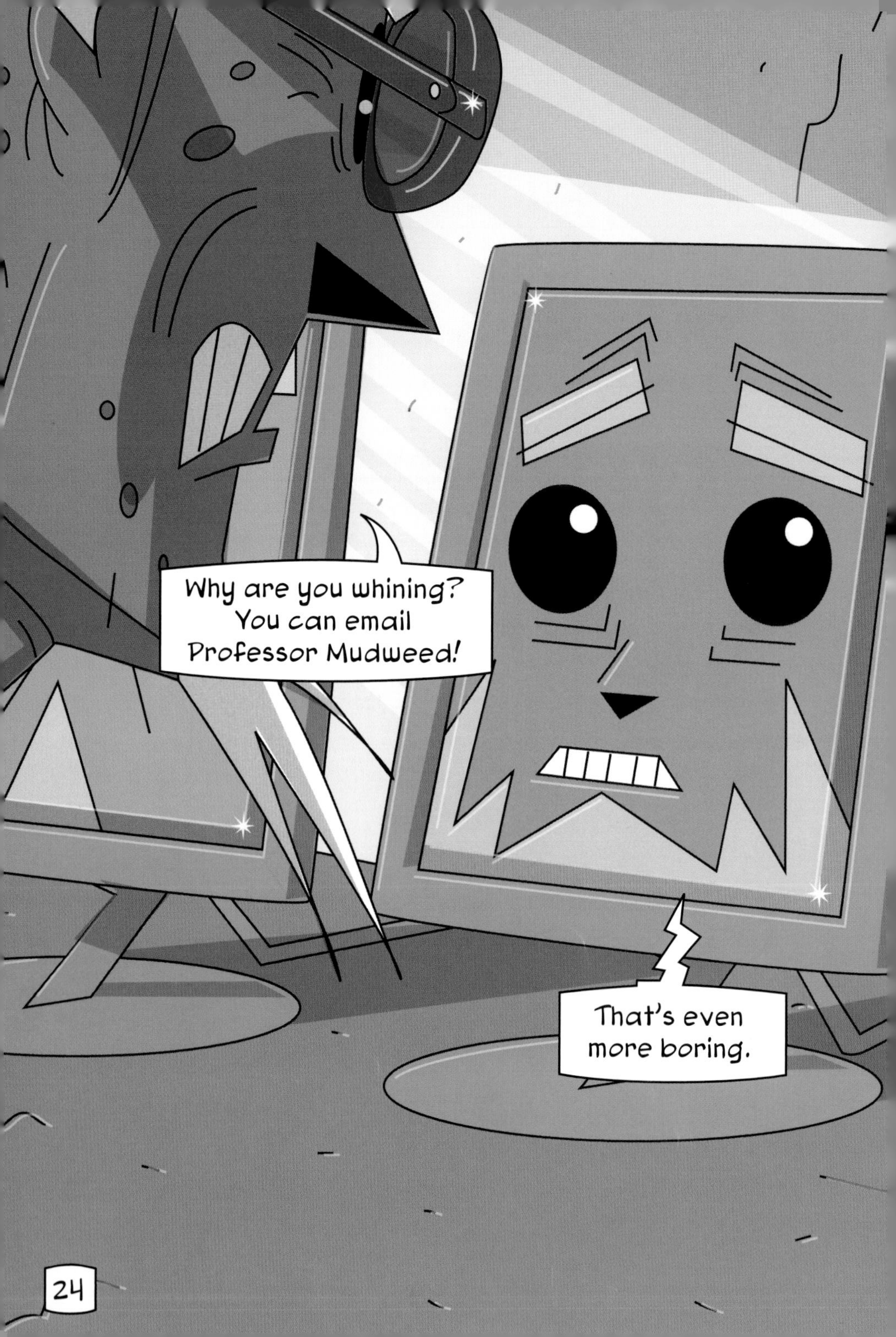
Why are you whining? You can email Professor Mudweed!
That's even more boring.

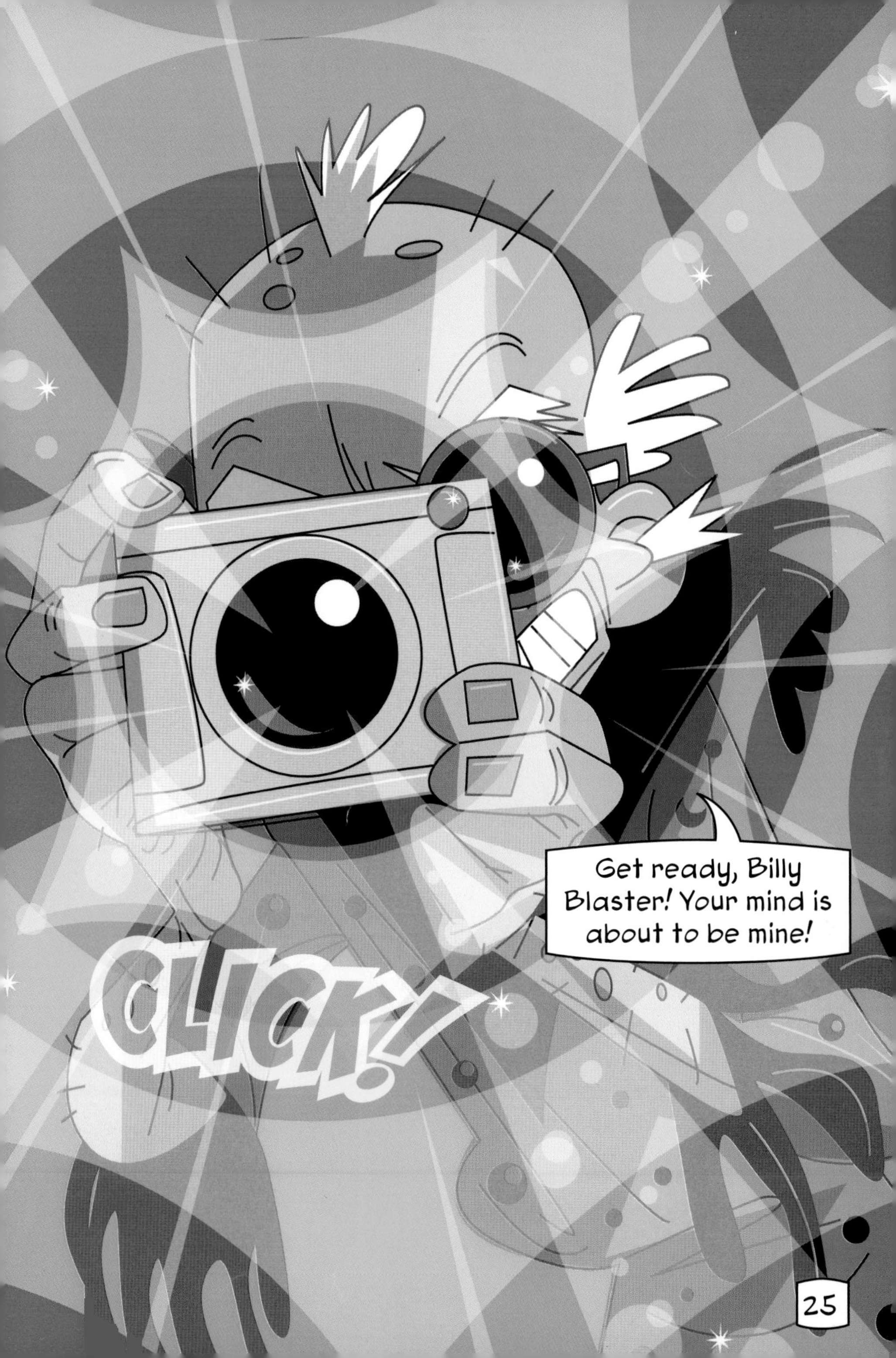
Get ready, Billy Blaster! Your mind is about to be mine!
CLICK!

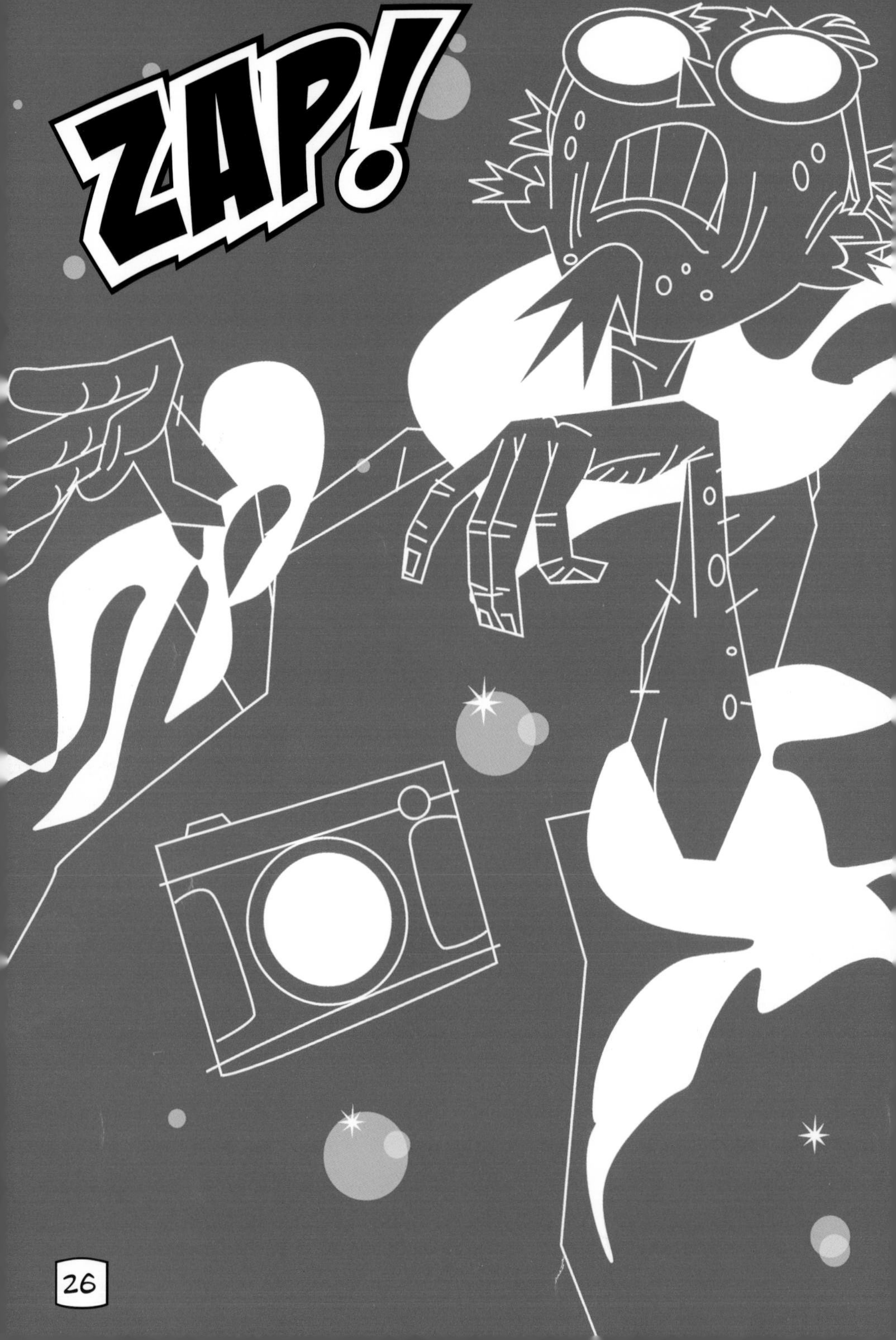
ZAP!

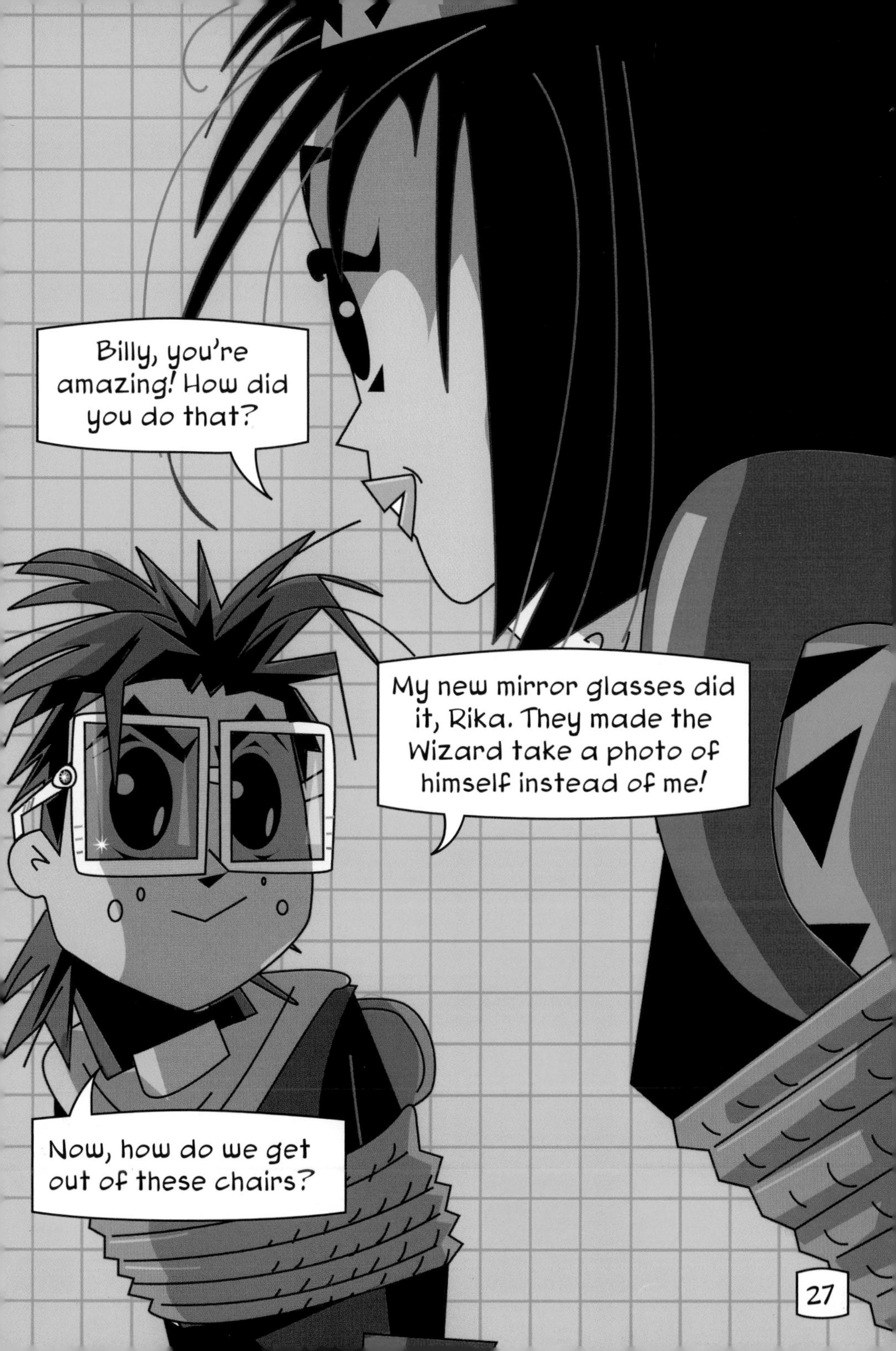

Billy, you're amazing! How did you do that?
My new mirror glasses did it, Rika. They made the Wizard take a photo of himself instead of me!
Now, how do we get out of these chairs?

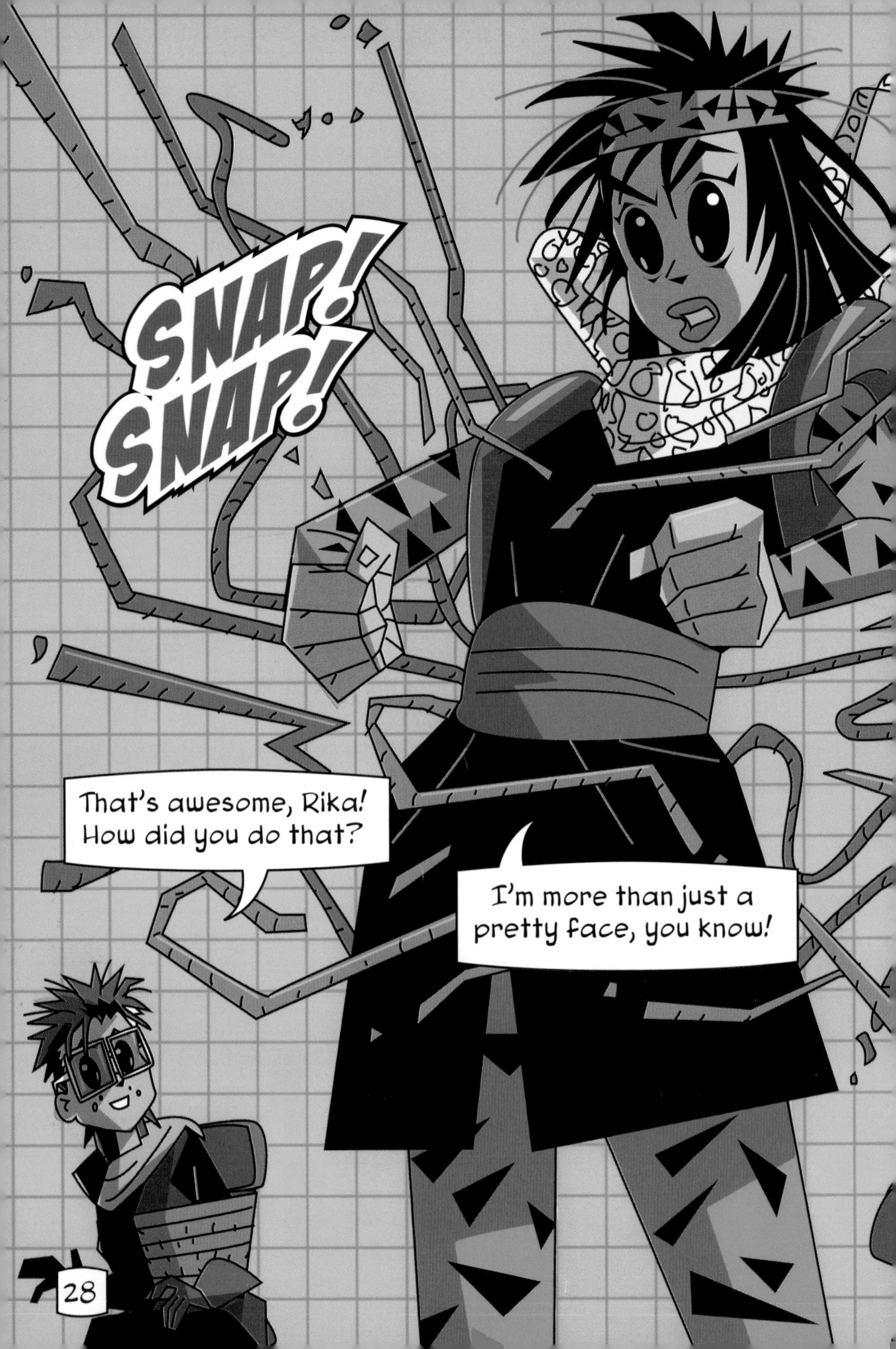
SNAP! SNAP!
That's awesome, Rika! How did you do that?
I'm more than just a pretty face, you know!

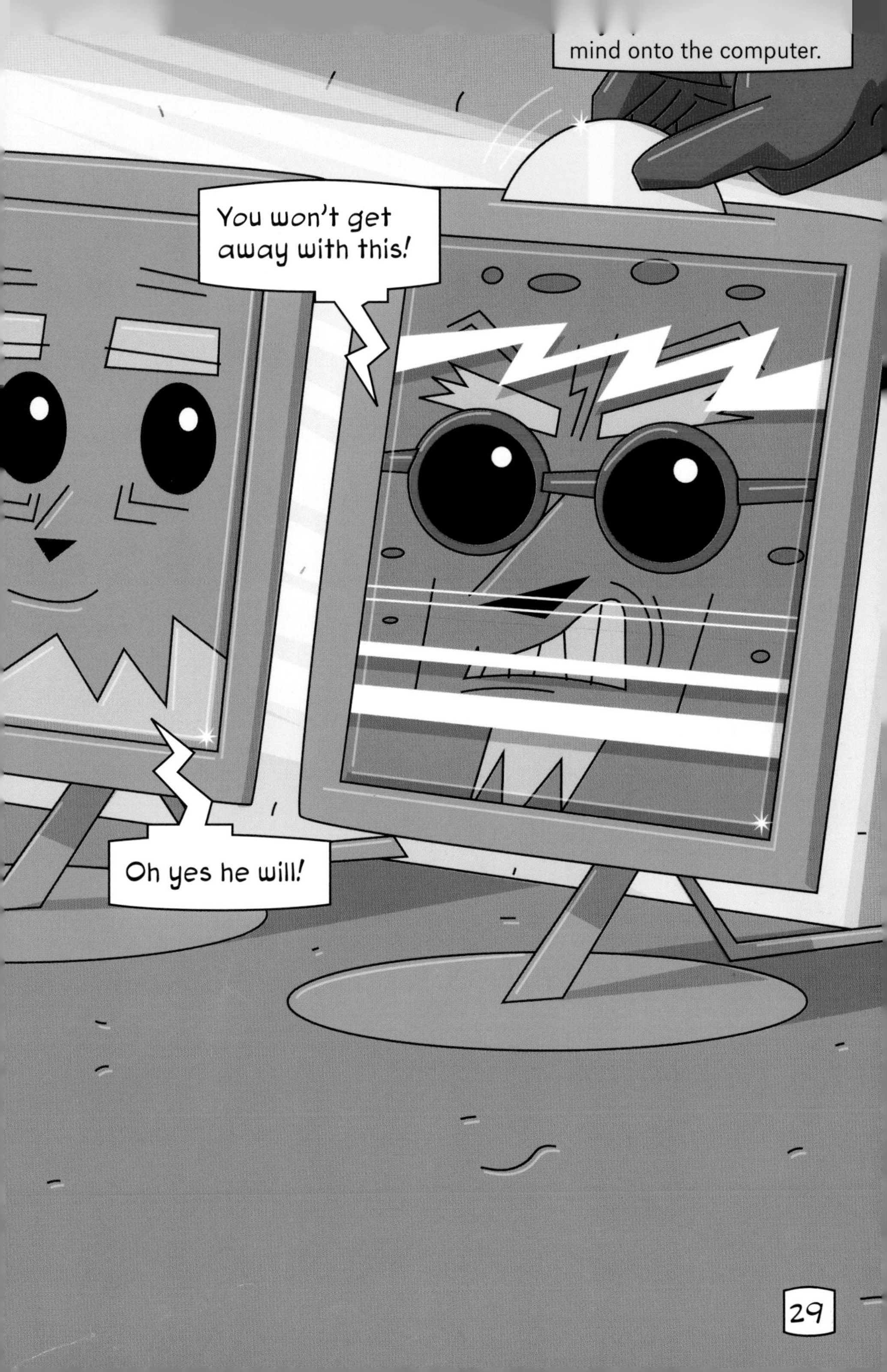
mind onto the computer.
You won't get away with this!
Oh yes he will!

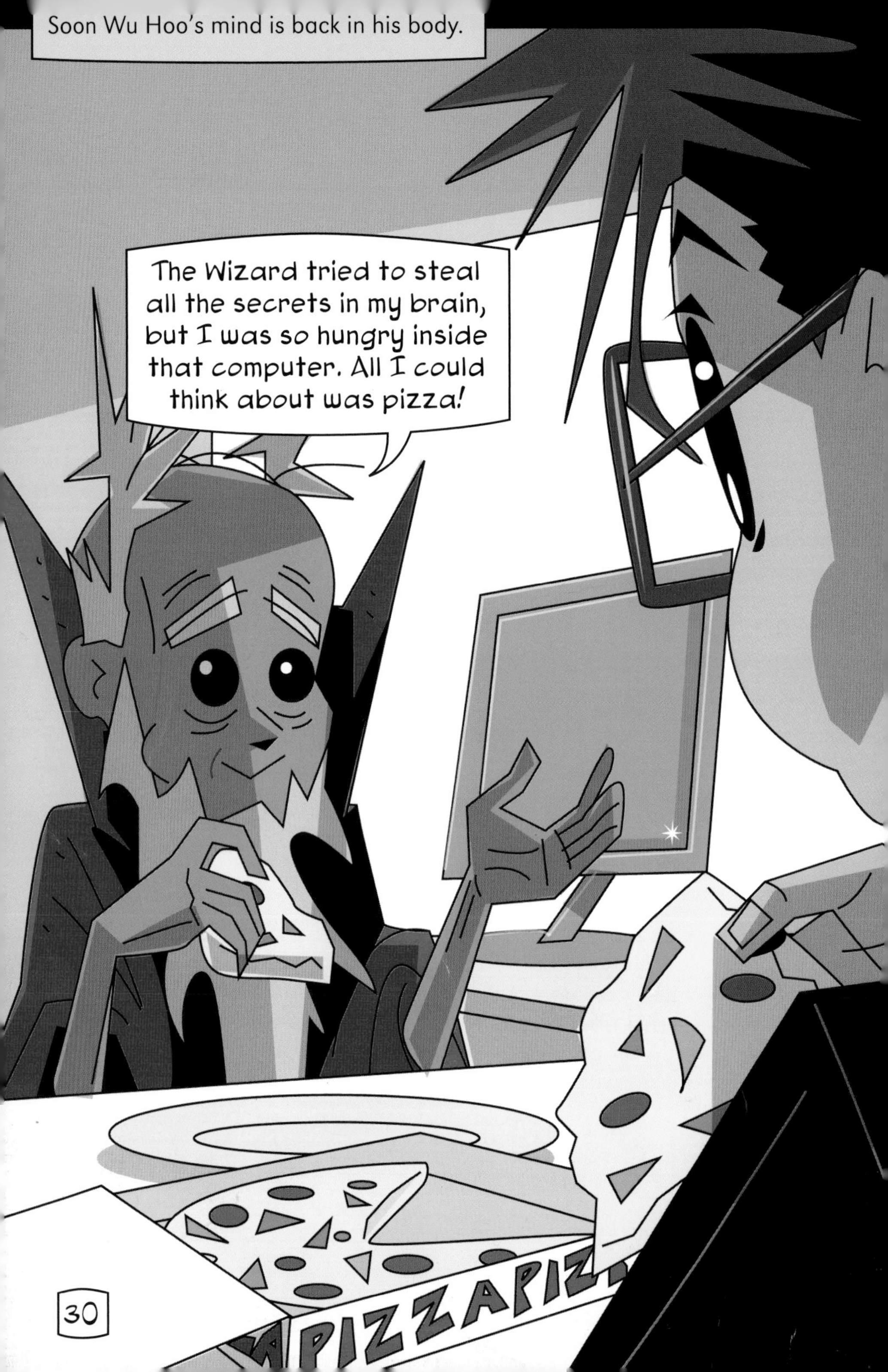
Soon Wu Hoo's mind is back in his body.
The Wizard tried to steal all the secrets in my brain, but I was so hungry inside that computer. All I could think about was pizza!
PIZZAPIZ

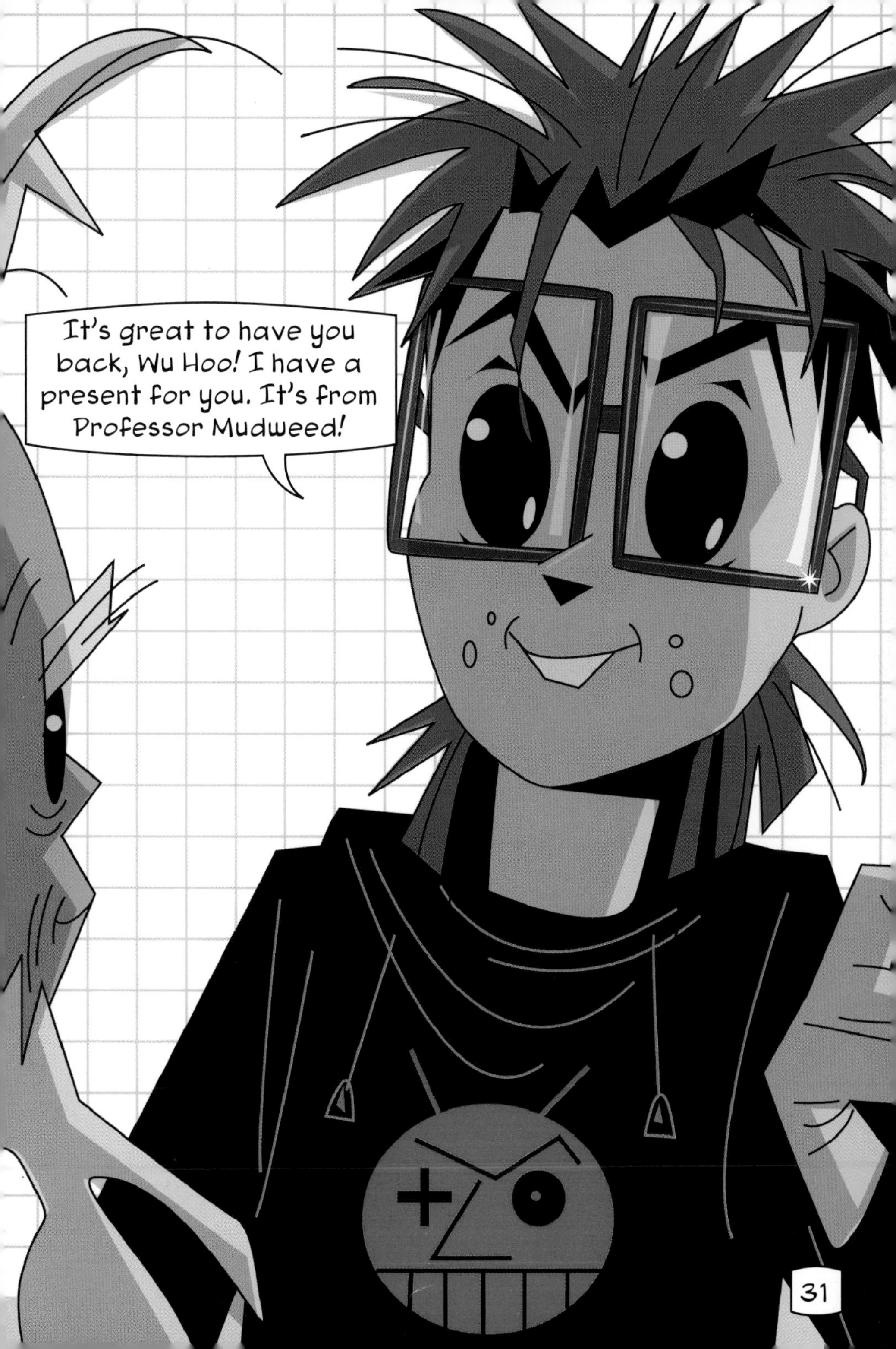
It's great to have you back, Wu Hoo! I have a present for you. It's from Professor Mudweed!

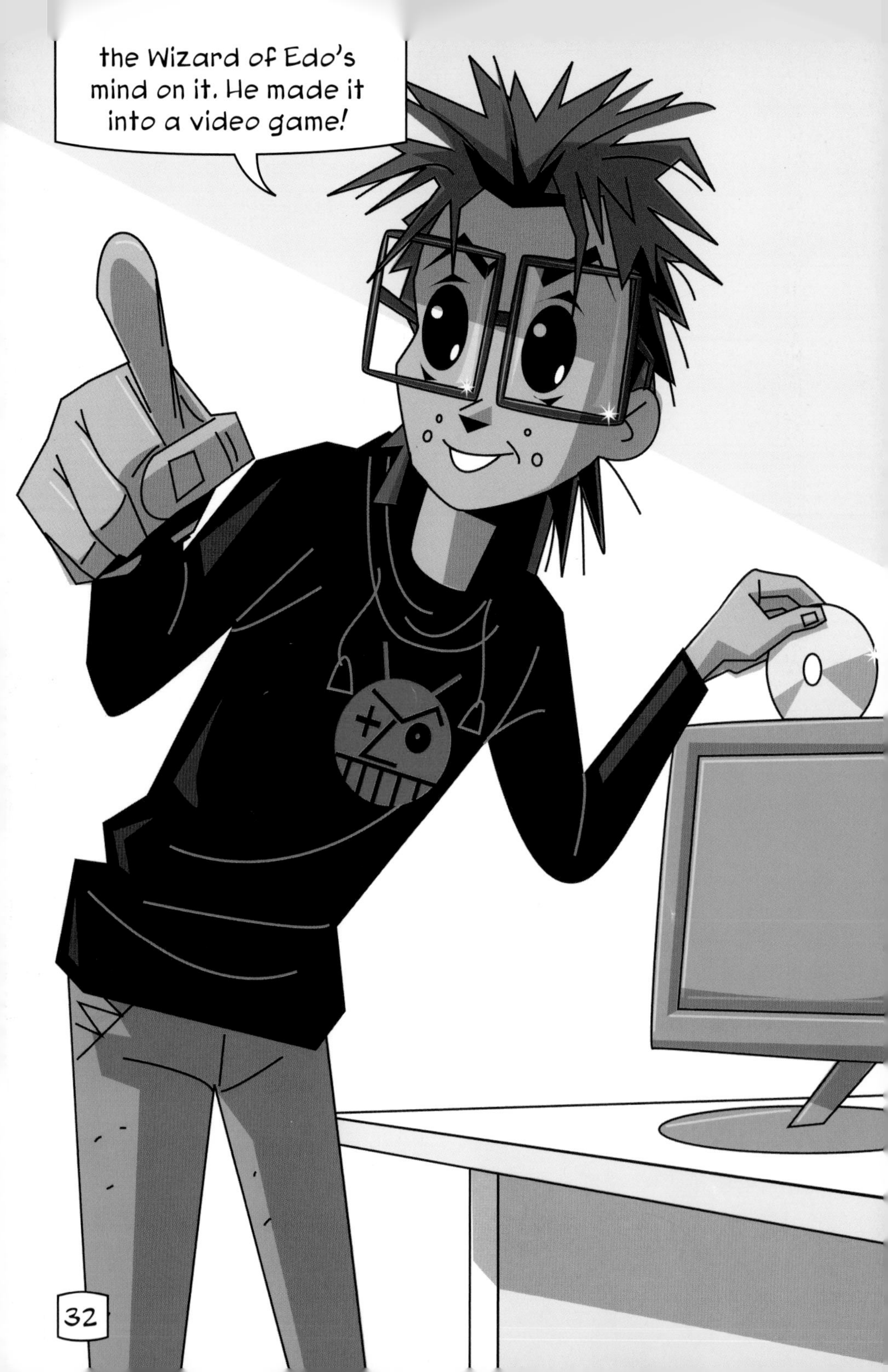
the Wizard of Edo's mind on it. He made it into a video game!

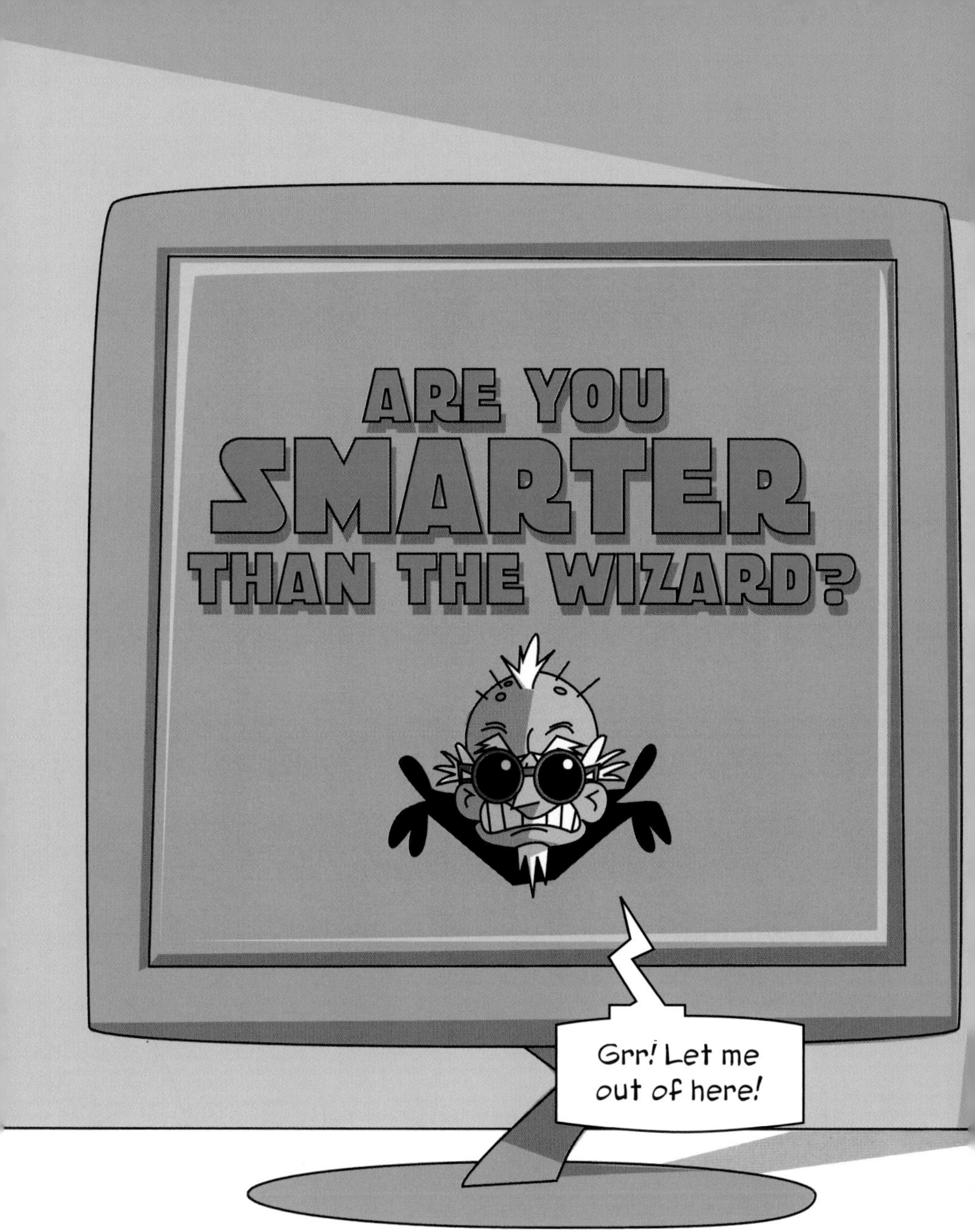
ARE YOU
SMARTER
THAN THE WIZARD?
Grr! Let me out of here!

ABOUT THE AUTHOR

David Orme was a teacher for 18 years before he became a full-time writer. When he is not writing books, he travels around the country, giving performances, running writing workshops, and running courses. David has written more than 250 books, including poetry collections and anthologies, fiction and nonfiction, and school textbooks. He lives in Winchester, England.

ABOUT THE ILLUSTRATOR

Peter Richardson's illustrations have appeared in a variety of productions and publications. He has done character designs and storyboards for many of London's top animation studios as well as artwork for advertising campaigns by big companies like BP and British Airways. His work often appears in *The Sunday Times* and *The Guardian*, as well as many magazines. He loves the Billy Blaster books and looks forward to seeing where Billy and his ninja sidekick, Wu Hoo, will end up next.

GLOSSARY

dangerous (DAYN-jur-uhss)—likely to cause harm or injury

expert (EK-spurt)—someone who is skilled at something or knows a lot about a particular subject

mind (MINDE)—the part of you that thinks and remembers

scientist (SYE-en-tist)—someone who studies science

trap (TRAP)—something used to trick or catch someone

understand (uhn-dur-STAND)—to know what something means or how something works

upload (uhp-LOHD)—store information in a computer

victim (VIK-tuhm)—a person who is hurt or tricked

whining (WINE-ing)—complaining about something in an annoying way

wizard (WIZ-urd)—a person believed to have special powers

MORE ABOUT PHOTOGRAPHY

- Some people used to believe that taking photos of people would steal their souls! People who believe in Voodoo think that doing things to a photo of someone will affect that person in real life.

- Most people smile when pictures are taken nowadays. But in early photographs, most people didn't. They had to sit or stand in place without moving for a long time while the picture was taken. If they moved at all, then the photo wouldn't turn out. How long could you stay completely still?

- Most of today's cameras are digital (DIJ-uh-tuhl). They store pictures on a computer instead of on film, like normal cameras do. Then, the computer can print out the photos. You can keep your digital photos on a computer for as long as you want. That way, you'll always have copies of your photographs.

- Cameras use lenses. A lens is like an eyelid. It opens to let light in, and closes to shut out the light. When a picture is taken, the lens in the camera is opening and closing very fast.

- The first photograph ever taken was a picture of some farm buildings and the sky. It was taken by a French man named Joseph Niepce (NEEPS). He had to hold the camera completely still for eight hours! That's a lot of work for just one picture.

DISCUSSION QUESTIONS

1. Rika is a super hero. What qualities does she have that make her a super hero? Does she have any super powers? What are they?

2. How does Billy defeat the Wizard of Edo? What else could he have done to escape?

3. Billy gives Wu Hoo a new computer game. What are your favorite games? What are the most popular games to play?

WRITING PROMPTS

1. If you were stuck inside a computer game, what game would you like it to be? Write about what you think would happen if you were inside your favorite computer game.

2. Billy and Wu Hoo both love pizza. What are your favorite foods? Describe your favorite meal. Then draw a picture of it.

3. Some people use cameras to make art. If you were a photographer, what kinds of things would you take pictures of?

INTERNET SITES

Do you want to know more about subjects related to this book? Or are you interested in learning about other topics? Then check out FactHound, a fun, easy way to find Internet sites.

Our investigative staff has already sniffed out great sites for you!

Here's how to use FactHound:

1. Visit *www.facthound.com*

2. Select your grade level.

3. To learn more about subjects related to this book, type in the book's ISBN number: 9781434212764.

4. Click the Fetch It button.

FactHound will fetch the best Internet sites for you!